To Tanjiel,

Saw this book in a little
Bookshop in Bosnia and
thought of you.
Here's to another year of
long, late conversations
about East + West, Love
+ Literature.
HAPPY BIRTHDAY,
Rozina 17.10.18
x x x.

MUHAREM BAZDULJ

BYRON AND THE BEAUTY

A Turkish Tale

Translated from the Bosnian by John K. Cox

istrosbooks

English language edition first published by
Istros Books
London, United Kingdom www.istrosbooks.com

First published in Bosnian as *Đaur i Zulejha*, 2005

© Muharem Bazdulj, 2016

Translation and afterword © John. K. Cox, 2016

Edited by S.D. Curtis

Cover design & typesetting: Davor Pukljak, www.frontispis.hr

ISBN 978-1-908236-28-9

Printed in England by
CPI Group (UK) Ltd, Croydon, CR0 4YY

Education and Culture DG

Culture Programme

This project has been funded with support from the European Commission. This
publication reflects the views only of the author, and the Commission cannot be held
responsible for any use which may be made of the information contained therein.

Supported using public funding by
**ARTS COUNCIL
ENGLAND**

LOTTERY FUNDED

Contents

Remember'd yet in Bosniac song.

THE BRIDE OF ABYDOS, XIII, 219

CHAPTER ONE

October 6, 1809

Dawn was coming. The rain fell softly. A flat greyness lay over the mountains. The city still lay in complete darkness. A kind of clear light, meanwhile, could be discerned on the far side of the encircling heights.

Byron had not had any proper sleep the entire night; he always slept worst when he was extremely tired. After three days of riding like the possessed, and three nights of sweet sleep under the stars, he could not fall asleep in a bed. Hobhouse was in the next room, snoring loudly. The other members of my party are surely asleep as well, he thought to himself, while I keep vigil like an eremite.

At first, it seemed that his bed was too soft. When he lowered himself onto the mattress, he sank in so far that, for a moment, he thought he had put on some disgusting amount of weight. He simply could not find the right position: either his leg ached, or he lay on his arm and felt it going to sleep, or he found himself lying on his back, his arms stretched out beside him like a corpse – but he could never sleep in that position. After that it seemed that the bedlinen was emitting an odd odour, but in reality it was quite clean: freshly washed and dried, it smelled like water and the powder that was used to wash laundry in these parts. Subsequently, he thought the ambience was too quiet. After all, this was a city, but there was no street noise; neither horses nor people were audible. Outside of the city, other sounds lulled him to sleep: the wind in the tree-tops, the roar of a freshet, the calls of the birds. But here the stillness was unbearable. In the end, he managed to settle down just before daybreak, blaming his insomnia on his own fatigue.

In his sleep, as in life, he was always at odds with the rest of the world. Insomnia had had the power to torment him since childhood. He would lie there in the dark all blessed night straining his ears and thinking. It was actually death on which he reflected the most. He was afraid of sleep; he was afraid of not waking up again. The thought of dying now struck him as less terrible than awareness of the final moment, but at the time there was nothing more horrifying to him than the idea of going to sleep and not waking up again. Once he heard his mother say that to die in one's sleep was a blessed thing, and yet he was appalled at the thought of such a fate. No, it seemed to him that as a boy he never once fell asleep without dread.

By the time he was fifteen or sixteen, however, things had changed. He craved sleep, but it came sparingly, and unannounced, like a beloved but unexpected guest. It was at that point he grasped the fact that fatigue could not lull him to sleep. He could be up on a horse all day long and then toss and turn in bed the whole night, tired as a dog but as alert as a sentry. Later, at Cambridge, his classmates would sleep best when they were drunk, while he on the other hand could not sleep a wink even when inebriated. Only a few times in his life, when he was dead-drunk, utterly wasted, blinded, was he able to fall into a strange, short sleep that was more like unconsciousness than slumber. Such sleep, however, never lasted more than two or three hours, and was usually followed by a terrifying, instantaneous awakening, full of irrational anxiety. He would be sweating, his heart hammering and his head throbbing with a dull, insistent ache. It was on account of such things that he did not enjoy drinking.

Even the act of love deprived Byron of sleep. Indeed, spilling his seed did bring gratification, but peace seemed to depart from him along with his vital male fluids. The sight of the sleeping body next to him was cause for envy and unease.

Suddenly, the *ezan* interrupted the stillness. The Arabic ode to the greatness of the one God reverberated in the ravines of the Balkans, echoed in the mountains of ancient Hellas. 'God is the greatest,' the muezzin sang, and Byron recalled a verse he had heard two months earlier on the island of Malta, when he had tried his hand at Arabic. An Arab poet, from the days when the banner of the Prophet flew over Spain, had written: "When the bird of sleep sets about building its nest on my eyeball, it notices the lashes and is frightened by the cage." Now that is poetry, thought Byron. Women had always told him that he had gorgeous eyelashes, long, shiny and full.

The call to prayer faded away. Morning, in its glittering white, had already conquered the room. The vague outlines of objects had regained their clarity. Byron resolved to stand up. He felt the urge to urinate, and the initial pangs of hunger.

Around noon the weather cleared up completely. With the greyish-white curtain removed from the clouds, Byron's mood improved as well. The sun beat down as if it were high summer, and Byron decided to take a walk.

He went outside by himself. Hobhouse was writing in his journal, but even without the excuse of journal writing, he was hardly likely to have joined him. It was the strange arm on a nearby tree yesterday that had unsettled Hobhouse beyond all measure. To Byron, however, it now seemed completely improbable that they had seen such a thing yesterday; it bore more similarity to a half-forgotten nightmare than to a fresh, precise memory.

After ten days at sea, their ship had put in two days ago at Preveza. The Albanian governor was there to greet them. They had no interpreter, but somehow they could make out that Ali Pasha was sending them his personal welcome via this governor. The name of Ali Pasha opened all doors hereabouts. He would be waiting for Byron, the famous English nobleman, in Yannina, according to the overwhelmed interpreter who had finally shown up from somewhere and who was clumsily putting together sentences in ancient Greek. Byron had not been able to refuse an invitation like that. While Hobhouse and his retinue made the trip to Yannina circumspectly, and against their will, Byron was quite thrilled about this portion of the journey: before them stretched a genuine *terra incognita*, of virginal, unknown and completely unexplored regions. Every third English lord or count had already taken a trip to Athens or Istanbul, but no one had been to Albania.

And the countryside was splendid, resembling the Scotland of his childhood – those landscapes at once rough and gentle that always reminded him of his grandfather William, that *wicked lord*. They had ridden for two days escorted by two gloomy Turks. Yesterday's dusk had revealed to them the silhouette of Ali Pasha's stone city that seemed almost rooted to the mountain. They spurred their horses and rushed forward as if returning home. They were already right by the city and the horses hooves were clacking on the cobblestones of the road, when a sight came into view that froze the blood in their veins. On a thick bough of a solitary poplar hung a human arm. A whole arm, long, which looked as if it had been ripped from a shoulder. It was moving back and forth like the pendulum of a wall clock, and the blue fingers were apparently lacking nails. Hobhouse and his suite averted their eyes immediately, and young Collins, one of the pages, had to vomit; but the two Turks were so conspicuously indifferent that it was obvious that this was a completely normal occurrence for them. It was a terrible, afflicting scene, but Byron was bewitched. He stared continuously at the dead member, at the almost beastlike, hairy underarm and the purple, bloodied upper arm, which was being picked at, slowly and patiently, by a raven of unnatural corpulence. The joy at reaching their destination had disappeared in a second.

In the main square of Yannina, a certain Hasan was waiting for them, a servant of Ali Pasha's. Once again a Greek person was found, and with his assistance they understood what Hasan was telling them; namely, that Ali Pasha was not in Yannina. Apparently, the ruler was sojourning somewhere in the north, where he had his adversary Ibrahim Pasha cornered in the city of Berat. He had commanded, however, that a house and servants and anything else the great English aristocrat might need be placed at the disposal of the visitors; he would endeavor to return as soon as possible and receive Byron in person.

They had ridden, exhausted, through a labyrinth of murky streets until they arrived at the house that had been prepared for them. A royal supper awaited them: milk, meat and warm bread. They ate rapidly and went immediately to bed, though for Byron a sleepless night was in store. In the morning a boy silently served them a breakfast that was exactly the same as the supper the night before, and after that they were left to their own devices. Byron and Hobhouse communicated in whispers. Although it was unlikely that anyone for fifty miles around understood English, they spoke so softly that they could scarcely hear each other. Hobhouse was worried on account of the arm; evidently he feared that his own arm might end up like that, but Byron reminded him of Ali Pasha's guarantee of safety. Hasan would come by later, Byron explained, and he'd most likely bring an interpreter with him, and they would be able to explain to Hasan that they could not remain very long. He'd be told to convey expressions of their esteem to the Pasha and they would then leave a nice present, such as the sword with the silver handle – and that would be that. Hobhouse seemed to calm down a bit and withdrew to his room in order to work on his journal, or so he said, while Byron felt drawn outside by the sunshine.

The streets were narrow and dusty, and the men on the street did not glance twice at him. Byron had the feeling that everyone knew who he was and under whose protection he stood, and that they were afraid even to look askance at him.

He took a long walk, ending up very far from the house in which he was lodging. For a brief moment, he thought he was lost and would not be able to find his way back, but he was saved by a minaret – that is to say, a white mosque with a tall minaret stood in the vicinity of the house, and using this to orient himself Byron found his way back. He had not seen a single woman in the city. And yet it felt to him as though women's eyes had been riveted on him from behind windows and fences, and from houses and courtyards.

At the house, his entourage was eating lunch. Hasan and the Greek from the night before were also there. The atmosphere was excruciating; no one spoke. Byron's arrival helped a little, with Hasan stating that the Pasha was likely to arrive in two or three days, but that Byron could continue his journey to wherever he wished and the Pasha would guarantee his complete safety. It also happened, Hasan informed the company, that tomorrow, or the day after, Isak, Ali Pasha's physician, would be coming to Yannina. Apparently, Isak could speak English. Furthermore, it would be no problem to obtain anything needed to make Byron's stay more pleasant. After the meal, they drank a full copper pot of boiling coffee and then Hasan left them.

Darkness settled over Yannina, and Byron sensed that this night was going to be one blessed with robust, beautiful sleep. The muezzin called the Muslims to another prayer, the penultimate, or final, one of the day. Byron was uncertain whether he should write to his mother or not. In the end he opted to wait a little.

❧

He fell asleep quickly and when he awoke it was still the middle of the night. This, however, was not like waking up after a night of drinking. He came up to the surface of sleep slowly and unwillingly, like a snared fish. He was lying on his stomach: left arm under the pillow, right arm pinned under his body. After a few drowsy moments, he realized what had roused him. His right arm had grown altogether numb; he could not feel it at all. That had only ever happened to him once or twice before. He thrashed his way out from under the blanket, flipped onto his back and picked up his right arm with his left, then waited for his circulation to do its work. Half-slumber enveloped him like a cloak, until his body jerked as if it had been scalded.

He remembered the arm in the tree. Massaging his numb right arm with his hand, he thought feverishly about that severed or torn-off arm. In the mute, shadowy night he was plagued by the question of whether it had been a right or a left arm before it became a scrap of dead meat. The seconds passed slowly. The numbness in his right arm dragged on. Then he felt a prickling on his right palm, akin to the feeling he got when, as a boy, he would press his face to his grandfather's cheek. Now the fingers were maneuverable again, and Byron opened and closed his fist anxiously. His arm rapidly returned to normal, and Byron lay on his chest again. He folded his arms and thrust them under the pillow as if he were preparing to swim away. Sleep, however, did not return so easily. As his eyes were closing of their own accord and he was gradually fading away, the image of that arm in the tree would rip through his mind just before he lost consciousness. He twitched a few more times, and then unexpectedly before dawn broke, drifted off to sleep again.

CHAPTER TWO

October 7, 1809

It was a cool morning. It seemed to Byron that he'd been woken by the cold. His left leg was peeking out from under the blanket, his foot was trembling slightly, and he could feel goose bumps on his skin. The day before it had drizzled constantly, but it had been rather warm; the hot breath of summer was still noticeable. But this morning, by contrast, autumn was baring its teeth. Heavy rain had fallen and the loud, even thudding of the drops called to mind a march. Byron was awake, but he did not yet feel like getting up. He didn't like autumn. He had never liked it. He once read a poem by that madman, Blake... how did it go? *"O Autumn, laden with fruit, and stained with the blood of grapes, pass not, but stay beneath my modest roof..."*

That's idiotic, he thought back then, and now it seemed even more preposterous. Accursed autumn, the damned change of the seasons, he thought; this is when the pain in my leg grows. There must be a catch in that phrase "pass not."

An odd smile passed over Byron's face. He remembered his first little book, those sixty-six pages to which he had given the title *Fugitive Pieces*. He loved the title more than anything else about the book, since it referred to loss, evanescence, or flight. He particularly loved that one short poem that still, to this day, gave him at least the intimation of an erection whenever he thought of it. But it was precisely on account of this poem that he had burned all the copies of the book. He didn't even keep a copy for himself, and he had carefully counted each and every one before the *auto-da-fé* in order to be certain, and he knew that he had torched all of them, but somehow, nonetheless, he didn't believe that this book had ceased to exist. He didn't know his own verses by heart, but he remembered the title, you see and he wasn't the only one. The thing still existed, therefore, although barely. Indeed, he had felt strange, watching the pyre on which his poems were burning. Present in those flames were also sparks of contentment: the book appeared to have lived up to its title. Its existence in the form of an object was, in fact, fugitive. He was fond of both the thin volumes of his verse that appeared later. Nonetheless, it would not have caused his heart any grief if somebody else had collected them both in turn and incinerated them. The vain bards of yore, who believed that a massive book could ransom their empty lives, would have lived differently if in their youth they had subjected their own books to the treatment he had given *Fugitive Pieces*. Fire teaches us about proper proportions, he thought.

A second later, he felt a strong stabbing pain in his leg. My damn old bones, he thought; no sooner do they cease growing than they start to break down. A man is like an apple – as soon as his cheeks redden, he drops to the ground.

Then words began to flash through his mind; as when you hear a few beats of a familiar melody – the whole world around you ceases to exist until you remember what the music is. New words are grafted onto the framework of the original ones. A poem. Byron recited it to himself in a whisper:

> *A drop of rain*
> *licks my eyebrow,*
> *like a suppressed and secret tear.*
> *It tracks across my cheek*
> *as the Rhine the continent.*
> *In a silent insurrection*
> *autumn kills the sun of my summer,*
> *just as the Achaeans did to Ilium*
> *in their wooden horse.*

Somewhere I have pen and paper, Byron thought; I have to write that down. And immediately another thought: why should I feel compelled to do that? Let it live in my head; it would be better for oblivion to devour it than flames.

Fortified by this decision, he emerged from under his blanket and sat up on the edge of the bed.

After breakfast Byron wanted to shave. A razor, as sharp as a sword, was brought to him, along with a jug of warm water and a large, lovely Venetian mirror. He liked to look at the reflection of his own face; he knew he had a handsome one. The curly, jet- black fringe, draped over his pale, high forehead. His skin had a distinctly white tone, like alabaster, and a woman he knew had once compared it to diamonds and moonbeams. He wasn't the only one who liked the scruffiness on his cheeks and the short hairs in his nose; he realized that the effect of his white skin was even greater when it contrasted with the black of his hair. His sleep-dimmed eyes seemed to show indifference.

Meanwhile, no one knew that his famous agonized look of secret mourning was the product of meticulous training. As a fifteen-year old, he had spent hour upon hour trying out facial expressions in front of a mirror. Women were transported by the way he looked when his eyes, as if irritated by the sun, teared up a little, and his brows tilted upwards towards his smooth forehead. His smile, proud and a touch contemptuous with its vibrating upper lip, was confined to the lower half of his face and did not extend as far as his eyes. A prominent nose, with a bit of the Bourbon about it; his delicate, chiselled lips, deep red, nearly purple; his teeth strong, with the narrow chin – the heart-shaped outline of his own face was thoroughly pleasing to him. He liked the way it gradually and evenly narrowed from his broad brow and protruding cheekbones to his lower jaw. It'll make a beautiful skull someday, he thought; yet it would be a shame for it to turn to dust somewhere when he could bequeath it to the Royal Theatre.

However, the visible hint of a double chin annoyed him. Since childhood he'd been inclined to corpulence. For him, boxing, swimming, and cricket had always had more of an aesthetic purpose than an athletic one. In the meantime, he had reconciled himself to the barely perceptible accumulation around his mid-section. His clothes concealed that, but a double chin was something much more serious. Ultimately I'm going to have to grow a beard in order to mask it, he thought. His neck was thin, long, and white, with skin even softer than his face, almost swan-like. His shoulders and torso were perfect. His chest held a thick clutch of black hair, stiff as bristles; then came his powerful arms, slender legs, and the disastrously defective foot. He was born with this handicap, and because of it he had limped since he could walk, but that wasn't the only agony that caused him to suffer: that crazy Bible-thumper, his governess May, who had deflowered him shortly before his 10th birthday, loved to tell him that he had no soul. 'The soul is located in one's feet, young master; wise people know as much. But you either have no soul or it is horrifically evil' – those were her very words. Much later in life, when he read about such beliefs in a book from the Greeks or Romans he wondered where she had picked up such information. She had also told him that he was the devil, that he was Lucifer, Satan, Mephistopheles, the fallen angel; for the devil – as everybody knows – walks with a limp, because of his fall from the heavens. 'He tumbled to earth and ever since then he's been lame. Your mad father sold his soul,' she said, 'and now you're paying for his sins'.

Later on, at Cambridge, he had plunged into learning Greek mythology, mostly on account of Hephaestus, the lame blacksmith to the gods. And they had something more in common:

they were both fatherless sons. While he had no memory of his own father, the man everyone referred to as 'Mad Jack', it was said that Hephaestus was born by means of parthenogenesis, which seemed to him like a heathen variant of an immaculate conception. Hephaestus's disability had been inherited by the Roman god Vulcan, and even the Scandinavians and Slavs had their own gods that limped. In his view, the devil's lameness belonged on this list: fire and a lame leg are what the devil inherited from Hephaestus.

Just as he was finishing shaving himself, Byron nicked himself on the cheek. He wiped a drop of blood away with his thumb and stared at the blade: it was as thin and keen as a thread of silk.

Hasan turned up for lunch in the company of a man with a red beard. This fellow was of medium height and average build, and was dressed inconspicuously. His face, however, was quite striking; with its thick, red beard, gleaming green eyes and regular but yellowed large teeth. It was a face impossible to forget. The two of them sat silently at the table. The Englishman finished the first portion of their meal – a thick, greasy vegetable soup – but the two other men had not even started eating. They began conversing loudly, presumably in Turkish, uttering occasional guttural laughs. Byron put down his spoon and pushed the plate away. He looked at the wall and started drumming his fingers on the table, waiting to be served the main course. 'Does the cuisine here appeal to you, my lord?' someone asked him, and, without thinking, he replied that the food was splendid. A moment later he comprehended that Hasan's red-bearded companion had addressed him in English. All the Englishmen looked over at him at once, as if by command, while Hasan and the newcomer began laughing seemingly without reason). Their laughter must have lasted for several minutes: they would stop for a moment, and then a glance at the dumbfounded faces around them would unleash fresh outbursts. At last they calmed down. Now Hasan rapidly spoke a few words to the new arrival, which the other man translated for him at once.

'Hasan *effendi* apologizes,' he said, 'and I add my apology to his. He tells me that he informed you he was bringing me here, but he didn't realize that you wouldn't know that I was the person you were supposed to meet, or that I speak your language.'

Byron suddenly realized that the man must be Isak, Ali Pasha's physician, and he almost chuckled under his breath. To judge from his clothing and all the rest of it, the man looked quite Oriental, but Byron realized he had assumed that a doctor with knowledge of English would more closely resemble a Londoner.

At this point the main course of roast meat and fresh cheese was served, and the conversation around the table livened up quickly. First they cleared up, once and for all, all the issues they had wrangled with on the preceding day. Indeed, they were told that Ali Pasha was in the north, subduing the disobedient Ibrahim, and that this matter would soon be resolved. They said he would be very pleased to receive the English nobleman and his entourage personally; both he and his son Veli Pasha, Lord of the Morea, who was sojourning at that time in Tepelena. In the event that neither his son nor Ali Pasha himself could come to Yannina in the next few days, he requested that Byron visit them in Tepelena.

'It is not far away,' said Isak. 'Just a couple of days' ride.'

Byron and Hobhouse looked at each other. Apparently Hobhouse was quite set on getting away to Athens as soon as possible. Byron, meanwhile, was happy at the prospect of an additional excursion on horseback across unknown land; and he was also interested in what kind of man this famed Ali Pasha, nicknamed the Lion of Yannina, would turn out to be. What would he look like, he whose fame reached all the way to England? Byron looked straight into Hasan's eyes and said that he was looking forward to meeting the Pasha and that it made no difference whether it was in Yannina or in Tepelena. Isak translated and Hasan rubbed the palms of his hands together and then stood up from the table. The two of them exchanged a few brief words and then Hasan left the room, leaving him in Isak's company.

'I'll be staying with you,' said Isak: 'I've been assigned to keep you company and to make certain that you want for nothing.'

Byron made no reply.

'Let's drink a coffee,' Isak continued. 'I need one, and it won't do you any harm.'

Byron asked himself that evening, when he retired to the quiet of his room, where Isak could have learned such good English. They had spent about three hours together after the midday meal, drinking coffee and chatting. Isak's English was excellent: fluent, supple, and somehow bookish. Admittedly, one did notice the foreign accent, but it wasn't definable. It was not the accent of someone from France or Spain; Byron would have recognized that readily, yet sometimes, when an English word escaped him, Isak would employ a French one. Byron wondered how many languages the fellow spoke. Their conversation today was fairly abstract and had touched only on general subjects. Neither one of them had dared to ask the other about anything at all personal. Nonetheless Isak had, at one point, asserted that he was a Turk and at the same time a Jew, and yet at the same time neither. Who is he? Byron asked himself. What is the story of his life? How old might he be? Judging from appearances, Byron thought he must be a little past thirty, but based on the amount of knowledge he possessed and the maturity that he exuded, he could well be twice that age. He liked Isak's deep, sensual voice. The man spoke slowly and deliberately. Byron's voice, in contrast, had something childlike or perhaps womanly in it. He had always been quick-witted, and the theatrical tone he had adopted in his early years in the *salons* of the aristocracy had unconsciously become a habit. Women loved the dulcet tone of his voice, calling it charming and magical, but here in the Orient, in the company of Isak, he came across, even to himself, as prolix and unworthy. He fell asleep that night with this concern on his mind.

CHAPTER THREE

October 8, 1809

As breakfast was ending, Isak cleared his throat, seemingly to draw upon himself the attention of those present, and said: 'Do not be frightened by the gunshots you will hear today.'

'What shooting is that?' One could detect the poorly concealed panic in Hobhouse's voice, but Isak explained that it had to do with a wedding. 'The lord of a small nearby manor, by the name of Zaim Aga, is marrying off his son. In these parts, people shoot their guns a lot, my lords,' Isak went on with a smile. 'But believe me, today's shooting is only the pleasant kind.'

Byron considered this warning superfluous, for a couple of bullets would hardly disconcert them. In fact, he might now well spend the entire day in anticipation of this event. Isak seemed to have guessed his thoughts.

'I'd like to emphasize, my lord, that you are going to be surprised by the intensity of this gunfire. It won't be the modest popping of a few rifles,' he continued, 'but rather a full salvo from an arsenal worthy of a real battle. You know,' he concluded, 'hereabouts the prestige and reputation of a notable are measured in part by the noise and tumult that he unleashes when his son gets married.'

After breakfast, Isak sat sipping coffee again, and Byron joined him. He was slowly coming to appreciate the importance of the thick, bitter, black drink to these Orientals. It loosened their tongues, brought them closer together, raised people's spirits, and apparently had the same effect as alcohol in the West, although it was somehow more elegant, and came with caution and wisdom both. It occurred to Byron, that after a few more rounds of coffee, he would be in a position to talk with Isak about nearly anything. Now, though, we are conversing just like two Englishmen: about the weather.

According to Isak, the day was splendid, and almost spring-like, 'God's gift to the wedding party,' he said, although Byron believed he heard a trace of irony in his voice. Byron said he'd enjoyed the sun, and according to Isak it was a good thing that he'd appreciated it so much, because the autumn rains were now, unavoidably, on their way. Isak sniffed the air like a dog, looked out at the horizon like a sea captain, and declared that this weather, was going to last for two or three more days, at most, and then autumn would begin in earnest. Byron just shrugged his shoulders.

'Indian summer, right?' Isak said after a short pause. 'That's what you all call this kind of weather, right?'

Byron mumbled something in the affirmative. It was hard to remain silent over coffee, he thought, and yet silence is a greater sign of intimacy than any other form of familiarity.

After they had finished off another entire *cezve* of coffee, Isak explained that he was going to be unavailable until the evening meal.

'I'm going to the wedding, my lord,' he said. 'I've been invited, and it's a great sin to refuse hospitality when it's offered. But unfortunately, I cannot invite you to join me, lest I abuse this offer of hospitality. It would be best if none of you went onto the street today,' he added as he left, 'it wouldn't be the first time that someone got struck by a stray bullet.'

'Well, it's my life', Byron mumbled under his breath, but Isak heard him nonetheless.

'Ali Pasha entrusted you to Hasan,' he said, 'and Hasan entrusted you to me; woe to him who betrays Ali Pasha's trust.'

Isak stood there thinking for a moment, before adding: 'honour, pride, vows, promises, trust, oathes – for all of that people here have one single word, and it rolls all of these things together into one. It's bigger than any one part and greater than the sum of all the parts: you should note this word, my lord. It is *besa.*'

A wedding, Byron thought, is such a silly occasion for a celebration. What poet was it who came up with the image of the marriage hearse? Only once had Byron courted a woman, and he had no intention of ever doing so again. Mary Anne, beautiful Mary Anne Chaworth, his kinswoman Mary. The first time he saw her he was just thirteen and she fifteen. His face back then was still smooth as a girl's, although several years had passed since he spent his first night as a man with his nanny, May. When they met for the first time, Mary Anne was taller than he. She was as beautiful as a goddess: slender and dark-haired, with budding breasts and curvy hips. She was his sun and moon and morning star, and for her he was apparently a tiresome little snot of a cousin.

Over the next two years they saw each other only infrequently and for brief periods. By his fifteenth birthday, though, things had changed. Then Byron was markedly taller, dark sideburns framed his face, and Mary looked at him differently. Meetings at a halfway point between Newstead and Annesley became a matter of course. They talked and were silent, laughed and cried over England, pouted and then reconciled. She didn't call him George, the way his mother did, or Byron like his friends, but rather used his middle name, Gordon. In turn, he thought up a nickname for her by combining her two given names into one: Marian. Lady Marian, as in the tales of Robin Hood. She was the first woman in whose company he didn't feel embarrassed about his limp, and she was the first who didn't ask him constantly whether his leg hurt, whether it annoyed him, or whether he was born that way or had hurt himself in childhood. The wonderful Mary Anne could slow her pace and stay beside him when they went on walks, so that he didn't have to strain, but she did it naturally and unaffectedly, as if she always walked that way.

Byron knew that she was engaged, but he never made mention of it. Engagements are a formality, he thought, but our love is a constant fire. Sometimes they kissed, on the banks of the river or under leafy boughs, passionately, fitfully, and abruptly. At times Mary Anne would simply push him away without a sound, but often she gave herself to him with the ardour of a lover who awaits her suitor after a year of separation. Her willfulness inspired him; never, neither before this nor later, had he experienced the same degree of excitement with a woman as when his lips approached hers. Coolness alternated with volcanic eruptions of desire; her lips would come close, as would the heavens for a great sinner, or they might open wide, like an unlocked chest harboring a legendary treasure.

For two whole years, he lived for the meetings halfway between Newstead and Annesley, and then one day at dusk, he asked his kinswoman for her hand. He was seventeen, and to his mind, a mature man. He would soon enter into his inheritance, and he was ready to marry his beloved. He had never considered that she might reject him and actually give herself to her fiancé. He simply could not have imagined that she would choose this John Masters, of whom they had together so often made sport – over him Byron, in the flesh. 'You know, Byron, that John and I are engaged'- those were her words. And Byron thought bitterly: I'm no longer Gordon, and he is no longer that mad and preposterous Masters, but rather John. 'So does this engagement mean anything next to what we had together?' he asked, and she shot back: 'Does what we had mean anything compared to an engagement?' That's when he knew that it was over. He tried once more to kiss her, but he regretted it immediately, even though she didn't push him away. Her lips, earlier so sweet and fresh, reminded him now of uncooked meat.

For days and months afterwards, it was as if he had lost his bearings. He didn't dare tell anyone what had befallen him. It was only the next year, when he and Augusta had grown close, that he could tell someone of that great love. 'When I recognized the hopelessness of this love, little sister,' he told her, 'I felt I was completely alone on the wide open surface of the deep blue sea.'

After Mary Anne he only indulged in embraces of convenience, rapid, frequent, and casual. But he supposed he would never again experience with a woman that swelling in his breast, when his heart threatened to burst; never more would his hands shake as they approached a woman's face; never again would his lips go dry just before the sweetest moistening. Never more would things be as beautiful again as they had been halfway between Newstead and Annesley. Never again… right up until Sintra. Sintra stood beyond compare: the most beautiful place on the globe.

He would write to his mother a letter with the following words: for me, the words *the most beautiful* now mean *the most beautiful after Portuguese Sintra*. Yes, Sintra was beyond compare. Its beauty surpassed everything that one could conceive of or explain. And that girl! When he first saw her, he thought he had before him the fifteen-year old Mary Anne once more, the way she had been when they met for the first time, or even more beautiful. She wore a spotless dress of white linen, with her dark brown, half-African face, and her small nose with the wide nostrils that imparted a sense of immediacy, and her worldly eyes full of health and merriment. She greeted him with words he could not understand, and quite bashfully, but in her voice and movements was something more than a usual greeting, although he knew not what it was. Her body rocked gently back and forth and she smiled at him, looking directly into his eyes, all the while wetting her dry lips with her tongue. Nothing is more arousing than lips like those. They had something of the world of plants and minerals about them. Irregular, like fruit accidentally split open, they showed what hot, dark, sweet blood comprised the inside of the mature little body. Only in the corners of the mouth were her sculpted lips drawn tight, as in a woman of the Caucasian race, but even these corners disappeared into indeterminate shadows, like the petioles of a leaf. They looked at each other for a long time, and Byron sank into her topaz pupils. They circled around each other, but nothing else happened. Voices crashed into their trance-like state, and Byron turned away, almost at a run.

This brief encounter made more of an impression on him than anything since Mary Anne. Over and over he thought about the girl from Sintra, and in his mind he called her "little creature." This obsession was not always the most pleasant of things, and he attempted to get rid of it by hurling himself into the arms of Lady Spencer Smith, the Circe of our enchanted island. She was a fascinating woman, the daughter of the Austrian ambassador in Istanbul, who combined the elegance of the West with the Eros of the East in her person. But it didn't work. As the voluptuous woman came noisily to her climax, Byron's thoughts were in Sintra. Coincidentally, at the same time all of Yannina was booming with hundreds of gun-shots, and all the members of his retinue pressed themselves against the walls like frightened animals.

Long after night had fallen, the door squeaked quietly. Byron was sitting alone at the table in the light of an oil lamp. Isak very nearly tripped over his own feet as he entered. It seemed he has had something stronger than coffee to drink, Byron mused.

'You are awake, my lord,' Isak said, almost light-heartedly. 'I thought you'd be asleep.'

'I was hoping to write a few letters,' replied the Englishman, 'but in the end I couldn't bring myself to do it.'

Isak joined him at the table.

'How was the wedding?' Byron asked.

'It was a wedding like any other, my lord. A wedding like any other.' He fell into a brief silence, and then asked softly, 'You are young, my lord, yet you are not married?'

Byron shook his head, and, in this fraction of a second a thought ran through his mind. Outside of Albania, he mused, I will never again meet this Isak anywhere; therefore there's no reason not to be as honest with him as I am with myself.

'I have not married,' said Byron, 'although four years ago I hoped to do so.'

Then he looked him straight in the eye and told him, rapidly, as if he feared he might change his mind, the whole story of Mary Anne and the girl from Sintra. Isak knew how to listen: he interjected not a single word, and his facial gestures showed that he was listening intently. When Byron concluded, Isak merely sighed. They sat there without conversing for a few moments before Isak spoke.

'You know, my lord,' he said, 'this is really a beautiful story: painful for you, perhaps, but beautiful. You truly loved that woman, and this is not often the case. That's why women love you, too; they sense that you are capable of love. The fact that she whom you loved did not return your love is, if I may be so bold as to assert, of perhaps less importance. It is you yourself who have found love.'

With that suggestive whisper, Isak ended his short monologue. Byron's eyebrows rose inquisitively.

'Is there any way to discover love other than finding it oneself? Tell me, my lord,' Isak inquired, 'how many men courted your esteemed kinswoman?'

'Two,' Byron replied, 'Masters and I.'

'Ah, the West,' Isak said, smiling ambiguously. 'Even in love, you make the calculations. Here in the Orient, he went on, a girl who is even halfway attractive has dozens of suitors. This Leila, who at this very moment' and here he rubbed his hands together lasciviously, 'is probably being deflowered by Ahmed, the son of Zaim Aga, received proposals from thirty other men.'

Byron remarked that Leila must be a real beauty.

'She's pretty,' came Isak's somewhat indifferent reply. 'Listen, my lord,' he went on. 'You were very forthright with me, but I have not been completely so with you. I told you that I didn't invite you to the wedding so as not to abuse my host's hospitality, but I withheld the actual explanation. It would, for instance, have been no problem for me to take Hasan with me, although he was already invited. I could not take you,' and here he averted his eyes, as if by way of apology, 'because Zaim Aga simply would not tolerate the presence of a *giaour*'.

Byron looked at him curiously.

'An unbeliever,' Isak said: 'A non-Muslim. *Those people are giaours*. Make a note of this expression, my lord, for when you hear it uttered, people are talking about you. Zaim Aga would not have invited me either, for I am distasteful to him, but I once saved the life of his son. I healed a wound he had sustained in battle, after everyone else had written him off. Thus he is for all time indebted to me, and he forgives me for being an infidel. But I doubt that he would forgive a companion of mine. I wanted to confess that to you, my lord,' Isak concluded.

'There is no cause for concern,' Byron said in turn, 'but one thing still intrigues me. If he is indebted to you, then why did you still have to go to the wedding? If I understood you correctly, he would not have held it against you if you hadn't gone.'

Isak beheld him with bright eyes filled with what Byron took to be fondness, 'you are a wise man, my lord: so young, and yet so wise. Yes, he said, in this matter also I was not honest with you. Have you read that book containing the stories from *A Thousand and One Nights*?' he asked. 'You must have read it, for you are an educated man. You must be familiar with Galland's translation.' Byron nodded. 'Do you recall the story of Shahriman's son Badr Basim?' Isak inquired. 'Or the one about Ibrahim and Jamilah?' Byron didn't remember them.

'It contains a disguised tale about love in the East,' Isak added. 'Here we do not discover love ourselves. You asked if Leila is beautiful,' he went on, speaking faster and faster. 'Yes, she is a beauty from Yannina, but that's nothing. The whole land knows of true beauties; there is a certain Nizama from Tepelena who is known as such a beauty. Meanwhile there are other beauties, of whom entire countries speak.

In Shkodra, a good thirty years ago, there was raven-haired Belkisa, who had hundreds of wooers but finally took up with Ali Pasha. She died giving birth to Veli Pasha. Once in Thessaloniki there was Rahel, a Jewess, who made the old man Bilal Pasha and his five sons lose their minds. Eventually, she drowned herself in the harbour like Aegeus. No one knows why, although people say it was on account of her beauty. And a long while ago, Sarajevo had Katinka, about whom people sang songs while she still lived; for her, not even Djerzelez Alija – a figure like Robin Hood in your country – was good enough. Once every three hundred years there is born a beauty who becomes known throughout the entire Empire. And then we live those stories from *A Thousand and One Nights*. Men fall in love with these women by hearsay alone. Nobody, or almost no one, has ever seen one of these women, but every man in the Empire daydreams of one of them, and is sure he would recognize her the moment he laid eyes on her – from the beardless Roma youths right up to the Sultan himself. She's a beauty of the order of the city Sintra you were talking about; no one could invent her, or dress her in the right words, but she is lovlier than any city, because she's a living being. You also know that a woman such as this truly exists, because no one could invent her. One may well be able to describe her in metaphors: hair as dark as a night of farewell, a face as beautiful as a whole day of ecstasy, eyes as blue as the sky in May, globes of ivory for breasts, hips as powerful as the crown of a tree, and feet like spearheads. But words are nothing, my lord.

It is a splendid thing to be born at a time when a woman like this treads the earth, let alone appears before our eyes. That is the reason I went to the wedding, my lord. It was rumored that such a woman would be in attendance; since she's a relative of some sort of the unfortunate bridegroom, Ahmed. But she did not come, and perhaps it's better that way.'

A bit out of breath, Isak paused momentarily and then added, 'It's time to go to sleep, my lord.'

'Why now?' Byron asked.

'Ask me no more,' Isak said, 'for I can talk no more tonight, my lord, but perhaps tomorrow. Morning brings fresh counsel.'

'Very well,' said Byron. 'But at least reveal her name to me.'

'Zuleiha.'

CHAPTER FOUR

October 9, 1809

Another sleepless night: Byron lay awake until morning, looking up at the ceiling. But anyone in the same room with him would have believed him to be sleeping. He did not move, neither turning from side to side nor sitting up nor rising; no, he lay there quietly on his back and stared at the ceiling. 'Zuleiha,' he repeated to himself. 'Zuleiha!' His lips formed the word silently. Three syllables: *zu lei ha*. *Zu*: the incisors in his mouth clicked briefly to make the sound. *Lei*: the tip of his tongue flitted over his teeth. And *ha*: his lower lip leapt out as if he were amazed. Oh, how tenderly had Isak pronounced this name! Byron doubted he could do the same.

The local vocabulary and names that had somehow worked their way into Isak's English possessed a special power. Besa – a word as hot, crackling, and glowing as a flame; giaour – a word as secretive and menacing as a concealed dagger; Zuleiha – a name as rich and multi-layered as life itself, mixed with indolence and serendipity. Can one fall in love, Byron wondered, with a word, or with a name? Does a rose by any other name truly smell as sweet? Would Isak's story last night have had such an effect on him if, at the end of the conversation, he had uttered a different, but equally beautiful and exotic, name? In his mind he went intently back over every detail of his talk with Isak. Was it not accurate to say that his interlocutor seemed a little drunk? How was it even possible to get drunk at a Muslim wedding, particularly if the father of the bride was such a zealot? Where was Zuleiha supposedly from? 'She's known throughout the entire Empire,' Isak had said. Byron was thus convinced that she was not Albanian. Isak had not said

33

anything about her origin, but the announcement of her arrival would hardly have sparked so much excitement if she hailed from the immediate vicinity. Also, the delay spoke in favour of Byron's thesis. Zuleiha comes from afar, Byron thought, from a great distance indeed, from one of those regions and landscapes in whose names the magic of her name is matched.

When it gradually began to get light outside, Byron swore that he would see Zuleiha for himself. At least catch a glimpse of her. The vow calmed him. The morning had already broken when a deep, fortifying sleep briefly overcame him, akin to a drink of cold water. He woke up quickly, much refreshed, and he felt as though he had slept the entire night through. He stood up and dressed. He was cheerful, hungry, and impatient. He supposed Isak had already risen, since it was likely he slept no longer than usual despite the drink he had enjoyed the night before, and was already up and active. He hurried to the refectory with that same nearly forgotten feeling of joyous expectation with which he once hurried towards Annesley.

When Byron walked in, Isak was already eating breakfast. His impression was of one who had also slept poorly: his hair was disheveled, his eyes were a bit red, and pearls of sweat stood out on his forehead. Isak looked so odd that even Byron thought he'd fallen prey to a fever. His voice was hoarse when he wished Byron a good morning. Byron himself mumbled a passing pleasantry as he sat down. Actually, he wanted to ask Isak how he'd slept, and to wish him a pleasant morning and a good breakfast, but only by way of a necessary introduction to what he really wanted: to request that Isak tell him all he knew about Zuleiha. But Isak was the first to speak.

'Forgive me, my lord,' he began. 'I talked a lot yesterday. Too much, like a woman.' Byron felt as though cold water had been dumped over his head. After a short pause, he replied: 'I enjoyed the conversation. It seemed to me as though we were both sincere and are on the way to becoming friends.'

Isak nodded his agreement. 'You bestowed upon me a great honour, my lord, with your story, but I failed to pay you back with the same currency. I was just babbling, my lord, silly stuff, which might have misled you.'

And for one short, terrible moment, Byron believed that Isak's story from the night before had been pure fantasy. The disappointment left him feeling as if he'd been impaled. And yet, it appeared to him that Isak could read his mind.

'I invented nothing, my lord. I was just in a lyrical mood, and poets are fools – surely we agree on that point.'

Byron gave a laugh, wordless but bitter, and Isak went on.

'Zuleiha exists, and she is the most beautiful woman in the Empire, but it's better to speak of her in ordinary language and simple words. Just in and of itself, her beauty is amazing, and she has no need of ornamental odes.'

After saying this, Isak fell silent again. Indeed Byron was worried that he was going to have to draw the words out of Isak this morning like buckets of water out of a well, but he was mistaken. Isak hesitated for another brief moment, and then he started to speak again.

'She comes from Bosnia, my lord, and those Bosnians cannot speak about anything without using the words *dert* and *sevdah*. And this includes love.'

Once more, two unusual words had made their way into Isak's smooth English: *dert* and *sevdah*.

'My lord,' Isak continued, '*dert* and *sevdah* are one and the same thing and yet different. They mean yearning, they mean craving, and love and burning desire and mania and passion; they mean ecstasy, they mean sighing, and they mean fire. *Dert* is red like blood, and *sevdah* is as black as gall. *Dert* is a wounded wolf, while *sevdah* is a flower that is withering. And *dert* and *sevdah* are songs. *Dert* sings loudly, and *sevdah* softly – because the Bosnians must always have their songs. And a song for them, my lord, is what it used to be everywhere: words and music. The Bosnians know nothing of sonnets and other poems; a song is something that is sung, and what one sings of is beauty.'

Where is this place called Bosnia?' Byron inquired.

Isak pointed towards the mountains. 'North of here, and to the west,' he said: 'A stern and beautiful land. I spent my youth there. It is a perfect land, as a Turk once told me; wherever you dig, up comes potable water, and wherever a seed falls, there a tree will sprout. Nowhere is the water any sweeter, or the shade any more beautiful, my lord. This place you were speaking of, my lord, this Sintra, seems to me to be complete *sevdah*, but Bosnia is at once *sevdah* and *dert*.'

Byron shrugged his shoulders as he reflected.

'You know, my lord,' Isak added, 'I don't know much more about Zuleiha than what I told you last night, but she is currently somewhere in this vicinity and it is quite probable that we will both catch a glance of her. Meanwhile, I still owe you a story about myself, because yesterday evening you were very honest and forthright with me. If I were to fail to talk more, it would be ungracious of me. The night is better suited for such conversations, so I hope it won't disturb you if we wait till evening.'

Byron agreed with a nod of his head. 'Just tell me one thing,' he whispered, 'if you know it. This name "Zuleiha" – what does it mean?'

Isak smiled. 'Do you recall the beautiful Egyptian woman in the Bible, he asked. 'The one who seduced Joseph?'

Byron said that he remembered.

'Well, Isak continued, in the Koran that woman's name is Zuleiha. There is much conjecture about the meaning of her name. But supposedly it means "the one who withdraws" or "she who slips through your fingers".'

'My father,' Isak began, as the candle sputtered in the background, 'was a rabbi in Amsterdam. I am, my lord, the child of weak loins. My father was already over fifty-years old when I was born. My mother was not yet sixteen, but I have no real memories of her because she died right around the time I was weaned. My father, incidentally, was a genuine *Wandering Jew*: I know that he lived in Budapest, Prague, Berlin, Istanbul, and London. He was a distant relative of the famous London rabbi David Nieto. My father's sister, my Aunt Deborah, lived with us after the death of my mother. It was with her that I first spoke English. In turn she also passed away, before my twelfth birthday. My father had long been fed up with Amsterdam and was looking for a chance to leave. I don't know how it all came to pass, but one day he departed for Turkey, only this time not to Istanbul but to Bosnia: to Sarajevo, where he would serve as a rabbi. And I moved with him.'

Isak spoke in clipped, spare phrases, like an encyclopedia entry, or as if he were retelling material that he had memorized, rather than recalling his own life. But with his arrival in Bosnia, the report got richer in colour and detail. With much ardour he told of foaming rivers, blossom-covered plum orchards, lonely fortresses, grey-coloured mountains, foggy bottom-lands, muddy roads, steep mountain villages and airy forests.

'All of Bosnia is riddled with canyons, my lord, like the wrinkles on an old man's brow. The rivers there gleam blue and green, like the eyes of Slavic beauties of old, and alongside them twist old, narrow roads, blazed by time and history. Wherever a gorge affords you a wider view, the lights of a city shine forth: ancient, terraced, pocket-sized, and lovely.'

That's how Isak spoke of Bosnia. Authentic *sevdah* gripped him as he began to speak of Sarajevo, and Byron was reminded again of that word. His very voice grew more resonant. Wax ran down the side of the thick candle like giant, heavy tears, and Isak talked himself into a fever pitch.

'When it rains in Sarajevo,' he said, 'it's like a transparent curtain of silk; when it snows, it's as if someone is plucking a whole flock of white geese; when it's sunny there, the sky gleams like gold and is as hot as coals – hot enough to melt stone. In Sarajevo, the wind blows mercilessly, pushing everything before it like a sickle in the hands of a mighty reaper.'

It transpired that Isak had spent five years in Sarajevo, returning to Amsterdam when his father passed away. *Wanderlust* had sprouted in his soul, too. At this point Isak's tale grew spare again; he said only that he learned the basics of medicine in Germany, and that his travels took him to Istanbul. The candles were guttering by then, and Isak was in more and more of a hurry to finish his tale. He was speaking softly, almost whispering, and it was hard to understand him. He said he had converted to Islam, but Byron couldn't tell if he had done it *pro forma* and for pragmatic reasons, or if the cause lay deeper, in something more nuanced. For years it seemed, he was one of the most eminent doctors in Istanbul, until one day, out of a clear blue sky, he was overcome by nostalgic longing for Sarajevo. He packed up and made for Bosnia, but shortly before reaching his goal, he changed his mind and turned back. Yet he didn't return to Istanbul.

'To make a long story short, my lord,' Isak said finally, 'as I was on riding back to Istanbul, returning to my home, my route happened to go through this region, and I stayed. Ali Pasha made me an offer I couldn't refuse.'

With that Isak rose from the table, dipped his thumb and forefinger in water, and pinched out the flame of the candle.

'Neither, my lord, did you have Yannina on your itinerary. But here you are. And for several days now,' Isak said into the black of the night that had just swallowed the entire room.

CHAPTER FIVE

October 10, 1809

Beads of sweat, as large as peas, dotted Byron's sleeping countenance. He was rolled up in the blanket like a mummy, but his head was jerking – sometimes to the left, and sometimes to the right. He was dreaming. Ali Pasha was in his dream. Byron knew that it was Ali Pasha, although he had never seen this man in his life: an enormous, robust old man with a long, white beard, clad in a splendid robe of the type you see Orientals wearing in ancient frescoes. A turban graced his head. His face was identical to that of Byron's grandfather William, the *wicked lord*. The correspondence between Ali Pasha and his grandfather in the dream failed to astonish Byron. Nor was he astonished by the hulking size of the old man in comparison to his own smallness. He was not a child in the dream, he was already the adult Byron of today, but next to Ali Pasha he looked as tiny as a Lilliputian.

In the dream, Byron was trapped in a labyrinthine city: in a ghastly warren of intersecting grey streets, which were every bit as ugly as Sintra was gorgeous. The maze had several exits, so the problem actually lay not in locating a way out; the problem was the presence of Ali Pasha, who stood before every one of them. In the dream Byron approached him several times, and each time it seemed as if the old man was growing favourably disposed towards him. But as Byron drew close, the kindly face grew hard, peevish and stern, and his penetrating, censorious glance bored into Byron's eyes like a hançer or a blade of Damascus steel. Worst of all, Byron felt remorse, pangs of conscience, and the need to besprinkle himself with ashes without even knowing what his transgression was. Obviously some sin was gnawing at him from the inside, a sin unknown to Byron, but a goodly portion of Ali Pasha's power stemmed from this sense of secrecy and mystery. Faced with the old man's penetrating gaze, Byron searched his mind desperately, like an insecure schoolboy, but no matter how hard he tried he could not recall his crime. He knew that if he could just remember it, then all would be forgiven, his stumbles would give way to a stride, and the curves would be straightened out. Ali Pasha would step to one side, and in front of Byron the gate of the exit would open – but he could not remember anything. He stood on his toes and attempted, over the shoulders of the old man, to catch at least a glance of the light that meant open expanses and salvation. But he couldn't do it. The old man was too tall. All was lost.

Finally, he looked up at the face of the old man, in despair and contrition, beseeching him silently with his eyes, as a saint would do to Christ, the Redeemer. Ali Pasha returned his gaze. In his eyes there was no longer sternness or anger, but rather a sort of superior or merciless pity, as if the scope of Byron's misery was so great that even the evil, unfeeling old man could not take any pleasure in it – and perhaps also his gaze included a hint of barely noticeable indifference. The gaze cut Byron to the quick. He lowered his head and beheld the dirty floor at his feet. Above him a harsh and thunderous laugh could be heard; it shook heaven and earth and everything in between. It's as if a great wind is coming, thought Byron, in that opaque span between slumber and wakefulness. The wind slammed against his window. In his disquieting dream, he had cast off the blanket. Now he lay there uncovered, groggy and bathed in sweat. Dawn had come and gone, but the horizon was narrow and dark like the streets of the city in his dreams.

Before they started breakfast, Hobhouse had whispered that he needed to speak with him. They ate quickly and restlessly. Rising to his feet, Byron motioned to Hobhouse to follow him. They went out of the front of the building. It was cold outside: pendulous clouds clogged the horizon, and one could feel the moisture in the air, although the rain had not yet started.

'We're leaving tonight,' Byron said abruptly but softly.

'Where are we bound?' his companion asked.

'For the south,' Byron answered, 'towards Athens, towards Istanbul. We'll continue the journey as planned.'

Hobhouse looked around nervously. He walked over to Byron, leaned towards him, and nearly touching his earlobes with his lips, he whispered

'They won't let us leave'.

Byron wanted to say, 'What right do they have to detain us?' But he merely added: 'We shall flee.'

Hobhouse laughed bitterly: 'In these ravines and defiles we will soon be found, either by the Albanians or by death, and if they come to regard us as enemies, then I don't know which fate would be less desirable.'

To that Byron said nothing.

'I was not in favour of a sojourn in these parts from the start,' Hobhouse asserted. He looked all around and said: 'But now that we are here, we have to keep our heads....When in Rome, do as the Romans,' he said with an acid smile; 'and in the Balkans, do not stir up the wrath of the locals.'

Byron, looking pensive, agreed. Yes, for the moment he was enjoying Ali Pasha's favour. They had put a house at his disposal, along with everything else that he needed. That was pure hospitality, selfless and kind. Nonetheless, Byron knew that this kingly generosity could very easily change into its categorical opposite. He knew Hobhouse was right. But he was nonetheless tormented by his own subservience. He would've liked to imagine that he was remaining here of his own volition, but even the thought of Zuleiha did not help him in that. He knew very well what the problem was. He liked Yannina well enough; in fact, he actually found it pleasant but was unnerved by the correspondence between his will and that of Ali Pasha. Both of them wished for Byron to remain a while longer; but it irritated the Englishman to think that Ali Pasha might see in his stay an attempt to humour him, even at the expense of Byron's own unease. He felt the blood rise to his face.

He gave Hobhouse an urgent look and said: 'You are right. We should not flee.' And after a brief pause he declared: 'We will announce our departure, and then leave Yannina. Let us be off tonight.'

Hobhouse started to object, but the thud of approaching steps deterred him. It was Hasan with two attendants. When he caught sight of Byron, his lips formed a smile in the shape of a lateral half-moon. He greeted Byron in Albanian, embraced him, and led him into the building.

Isak was seated at the table, drinking coffee. He and Hasan had a short conversation, and a moment later Isak turned to Byron: 'Tomorrow we will depart, my lord. Alert your attendants. Ali Pasha has invited you to Tepelena.'

Byron caught the gaze of his friend Hobhouse, whose eyes were twinkling with laughter. Byron shrugged his shoulders. 'Tomorrow we leave,' he said.

ॐ

For the third night in a row, Byron and Isak had a long, intimate conversation. Byron had been occupied almost all day with the preparations for the continuation of the journey. Before dusk everything stood ready, but he knew that his usual case of travel nerves was still in store for him. He liked to be active the night before a trip; waiting made him nervous. He couldn't sit sedately when he knew that they would be back on the road the next day; he always just needed to bustle about, or at least throw himself into some task he had been putting off for a long time. Tonight he intended to write to his mother. He had tried several times unsuccessfully, and apparently he was not going to have any luck now, either. He couldn't even get past the first courteous formalities. Yet he was visibly cheered by Isak's return to the room. He enjoyed conversing with the man, and the fact that Isak would be accompanying them tomorrow made him happy.

'Good evening, my lord,' Isak proffered. 'Are you looking forward to the trip?'

Byron replied that his experiences of travel were decidedly ambivalent; he loved to travel, but on the eve of a journey he would invariably regret that he had decided to go.

'I understand,' Isak said. 'You, my lord, are a Westerner with the soul of an Easterner.'

Byron regarded him quizzically, and Isak continued: 'The Westerner has travel in his blood; the Easterner hates leaving his home. The threshold of your house, as they say in Bosnia, is the highest mountain. You will see this, if you haven't already: in the East, the idea of a journey for the sake of amusement is totally unknown. There are many people here now who are wondering what you're doing here. Some suspect that you were cast out of your homeland, while others reckon you to be a spy. A Turk only goes on a journey when he has to: because of the authorities – on a mission or into exile – or for the sake of his God, on a pilgrimage: The *hajj*, to be precise. You travel, my lord, because in the West there is a convention known as travelling. But in you there's also something Eastern, something indifferent and idle. You attach yourself to a country, one that need not be your home soil. You're not a nomad, my lord; you are not a John Lackland.'

With that Isak concluded his short monologue. Byron had to laugh. He sensed that Isak was in an optimistic and garrulous mood, so he ventured to ask him what kind of a man Ali Pasha was. Isak heaved a deep sigh: 'He is both lenient and callous, my lord, like all despots. The people, on nights when they are gathered whispering around the fire, tell both of his goodness and his cruelty. They are stories, my lord, of the sort you encounter in myths: Ali Pasha is a man with the strength of a lion but the soul of a nightingale; he bestows gifts upon poor children, but makes his enemies pay with tears of blood; a sad song might move him, while the cries for mercy of those who have set themselves against him are music to his ears; he honours women, yet lets his followers despoil enslaved girls and laugh at their sobs.

This is the perspective of the poor, superstitious, and uneducated peasants hereabouts, my lord; they've been living with such stories for hundreds of years, and only the names of the rulers change. Men like Ali Pasha thrive on the weakness of the Sultan; they are parasites on the body of an ailing empire. There are many such pashas, despots, and warlords in the wanton and bloody Orient. They are cruel princes who gouge out the eyes of their own brothers, castrate their own relatives, and live in fear of their own sons – all for the sake of power. For the sake of power, they plot and scheme with the devil himself; they do the dirty work of various higher lords, fraternize now with England and now with France, and then with Austria and sometimes with Russia, and they fancy that they are the equals of emperors and kings, even though they are actually just their servants, their dogs – dogs that assume that because of their long leashes they must be free. Ali Pasha is one of these modern, crossed unfortunates, a bad copy of Sultan Yahya.'

With that Isak was ready to stop his explication, but Byron shot him a searching look: who?

'Haven't you heard, my lord, the story of Sultan Yahya?' Isak was amazed. 'Then keep listening,' he added. 'It's a damn good story.

Yahya is the Muslim version of the name John. The Yahya who is mentioned in the Koran corresponds to John the Baptist in the Gospels. Yahya was the child of a Byzantine princess from the line of the Comneni and the son of Murat III. When the mother feared that her son might lose his life to intrigues at court, she sent him away to Greece; that is, to a monastery in Bulgaria. One of her faithful eunuchs travelled with the boy. The boy was baptized at the monastery according to Orthodox rites, and when he had grown up after a decade there, he left the monastery together with that same eunuch. They travelled the Balkans, disguised as dervishes, and Yahya was obsessed with the idea of becoming the ruler of the entire empire. On this account they nicknamed him "the Sultan."

In the following years, he criss-crossed Europe from Prague to Florence, from Venice to Paris, from Heidelberg to Antwerp, always on the look-out for support from the crowned heads of Europe. The Medici received him, and the Savoyards, the Nevers and Wallenstein, as well as both popes and emperors. He joined the Florentines on crusades in Syria and Kosovo. With the Austrians, he attacked Bar and Shkodra, and with Polish mercenaries and Ukrainian and Russian Cossacks he attacked Constantinople itself. He commanded a fleet of one hundred and thirty ships, and little stood between him and the realization of his insane ambitions. The unfortunate man probably did not realize, and also did not want to know, that his false allies in the West could hardly wait for him to fail, so as to take the chance to kill him and dismember his empire. Every local *bey* in the Orient dreamt of becoming sultan, but only Yahya made a serious go of it. All the others, including Ali Pasha, are just small-time robbers; they are weak and have no idea even of how to take a majestic fall. But decline and defeat are unavoidable for them.

Listen carefully, my lord, and remember: in the not-so-distant future, a sultan will decorate his palace in Istanbul with the head of old Ali Pasha.' Isak uttered these words in a barely audible voice.

Byron, grave and thoughtful, said nothing. 'Until then it is up to us to obey him,' he said at last. 'Let us sleep, Isak, for we both must travel on the morrow.'

CHAPTER SIX

October 11, 1809

They were not, however, fated to depart the next morning. They had barely woken- up, when Byron noticed they were in siege-like state. The horses were saddled, and everything was prepared for setting off, but the plan had changed. Hasan and Isak were having a vehement discussion, and the Englishmen were watching them bemusedly. Finally Isak turned to Byron: 'We will leave after the audience.'

'What audience is that?' Byron asked in confusion. 'I thought Ali Pasha was not here.' 'Oh, he isn't,' Isak muttered. 'You will be received by Ali Pasha's grandson.'

'Does Ali Pasha really have an adult grandson?' Byron asked.

'Well, how adult he is, my lord, is a question that would receive a different answer in the West than it would here. Mahmut Pasha is ten-years old.'

Byron was annoyed. 'A child,' he said softly, to himself. But Isak heard him.

'This is a not a child in the sense you are used to, my lord.' He sidled up to him and used his chin to indicate Hasan. 'See how nervous he is? This very morning Mahmut Pasha ordered Hasan to bring you to him, and he is consumed by the fear that you might give him the slip.'

'He fears the rage of a ten-year old child!' Byron exclaimed.

'He fears power, my lord, as everyone does.'

Just then, Hasan came over to them and had a word with Isak. When they had finished, Isak turned again to Byron: 'only you will go see Mahmut Pasha, my lord. I will go along as your interpreter, while the other attendants wait for us here. As soon as we return, we'll start the journey as planned, because it would not be wise for us to lose a whole day.' Byron nodded in agreement. 'When do we set out to pay our respects to the brat?' he wanted to know.

Isak gave him a strange look and said: 'Momentarily.'

The *konak* where Mahmud Pasha was going to receive them was only a few hundred metres distant, yet they had to ride there in a slow-moving procession, complete with escort. It was all that Byron could do not to laugh. There is something perverse in all this, he thought; Hasan, Isak, and he were going to pay homage to a boy, as if this were a parody of the Gospels. Their three horses walked next to each other, and they were accompanied by a troupe of soldiers: we are three abject wise men, thought Byron.

The guard who stood watch in front of the unprepossessing residence respectfully allowed them to pass. They then passed through a dim corridor, at the end of which a broad, bright room awaited them. At the back of it stood a luxurious settee. It wasn't exactly a throne, but it was a dignified seat for a ruler. On the settee two boys were seated. Isak and Hasan stopped in their tracks, but Byron seemed to know what to do. When he got near the centre of the room, the younger boy arose and came forward to meet him. He approached to within a metre or so, and then, with his right hand pressed to his chest and his head slightly bowed, he greeted him. Byron returned the greeting in the same fashion. Now the younger boy went back to his seat, and Byron repeated the ritual with the older of the two. When both boys were again seated, Isak appeared next to Byron. Hasan had disappeared somewhere.

'The younger one,' whispered Isak, 'is Husein Beg, and he's also a grandson of Ali Pasha.'

Byron barely heard these words. Awestruck, he kept his eyes on the two boys. Isak was right, he thought; children of this sort I have most certainly never seen. They were gorgeous: with dark skin, and even darker eyes, and facial features that were perfectly formed. Their lips were bright red. Clad in ceremonial garments, of the type that adult dignitaries wear in the East, they looked almost lovingly at Byron. Mahmut Pasha seemed especially impressed by the English lord: he looked him carefully up and down, from head to toe. Byron turned to Isak: 'tell them that I offer my respects to them, that I feel honoured by this meeting, and that I am grateful for their hospitality.'

Isak turned to the boys and quickly translated Byron's words. Both nodded their heads happily. Mahmut Pasha inquired how Byron liked Yannina, and Husein Beg was interested in knowing how big the country was over which Byron ruled. Byron gave cordial, brief answers.

'It is very beautiful here,' he said to Mahmut Pasha, 'it is smaller than the country of your grandfather,' he responded to Husein Beg. But the mutual affinity between Byron and the two was not a matter of words. After half an hour of more or less trivial conversation, Mahmut Pasha abruptly clapped his hands, and in a moment, a courtier appeared. Mahmut Pasha said something to him, and the summoned one disappeared again.

'May I ask something of you?' Mahmut Pasha inquired of Byron.

'Anything at all,' he replied.

'Could you deliver a letter to my grandfather?'

'It will be an honour to do so. '

Mahmut Pasha produced a scroll and passed it to Byron, who interpreted this as sign of leave-taking, and he prepared himself to make another bow. But the second appearance of the courtier held him up: he was carrying a bundle that he gave to Mahmut Pasha, whose entire face was now beaming. He made a short statement in solemn tones, and Isak interpreted it quickly: 'Mahmut Pasha has a gift for you.' The boy then revealed the contents of the package to him: a set of Albanian ceremonial clothes. Byron was moved. 'Thank them many times over for me,' he said to Isak.

Now the younger of the two boys got to his feet and bade Byron farewell in the same formal style he had employed at the outset.

Mahmut Pasha then repeated the farewells in like manner, but did not immediately sit down again. Instead, he walked over to Byron and kissed him twice on each cheek. When he had sat back down, he said a few more words. Isak translated: 'Mahmut Pasha hopes, my lord, that the two of you will meet again.'

'I would also like that,' said Byron, and then he and Isak withdrew.

Hasan was waiting for them in the corridor. As they were walking to the horses, he and Isak talked quietly. Hasan looked over at Byron from time to time with a mixture of envy and respect. When they reached Hobhouse and the rest of the entourage, Hasan dismounted and bade farewell to Byron with a deep bow. Then he remounted and quickly rode away.

'Here it is a great honour, my lord, to receive a gift from Mahmut Pasha,' Isak said, 'and an even greater one to be sent off with a kiss.'

Byron enjoyed being back in the saddle. The road was dry and fairly wide, and the weather was fair and, for autumn, quite warm. It felt good to be riding on this particular early afternoon. They left Yannina behind them, and the countryside showed fewer and fewer signs of human habitation. On both sides of the road there were sparse stands of deciduous trees with colourful canopies of leaves. The horsemen of the small squadron rode along in silence. Two Albanians rode at the very front, and a good twenty metres behind them, came Hobhouse, Isak, and Byron, and at the same distance behind them, followed Byron's attendants. The only sounds were the thudding of hooves, which blended with bird song and the fluttering of the wings of crows and doves as they flew overhead every few minutes. Byron couldn't help but think more about the two boys. Something about them fascinated him: it was their art-lessness, which was well-nigh animalistic. More precisely, Byron was dumbfounded that their patently strict and careful raising, the studied court etiquette, the ceremonial forms they adopted, and the peculiar stiffness of their involuntary early adulthood had not killed off the boys' curiosity, openness, sincerity, and child-like instincts. They are magnificent, Byron said to himself. Then a comment from Isak interrupted his meditation.

'I think it would be best if we did not stop to rest until the evening meal, my lord. We had a substantial breakfast, so we can skip lunch. We lost quite a bit of time this morning.' 'You are right,' said Byron.

'And there's one other consideration,' Isak continued. 'We should have been making use of every minute of these fair skies. I have the feeling that vile weather is headed our way.' Byron looked up. The sky was completely sunny; there were just a few innocent white cloudlets playing on the western horizon like a flock of sheep.

'I'm not so sure about that,' he responded.

Full of misgivings, Isak shook his head. 'You are mistaken, my lord. Up in the mountains, autumn will bare its teeth, perhaps as soon as tomorrow – at the latest, the day after tomorrow. That's why I want us to make haste...'

'So let our horses feel our spurs!' Byron declaimed.

They rode quickly and in silence as the sun dropped toward the western horizon. The horses raised up dust that hung in the air for a short time like a swarm of tiny flies. Byron felt hot, and so Isak's weather report still struck him as nonsense. But the new tempo suited him, and he did not protest. He wanted to see Ali Pasha as soon as possible and bring to a conclusion this unplanned stage of his pilgrimage through the Eastern part of the continent. When it grew dark, they reined in their horses somewhat, but they still did not stop. The moon was already shining down lustrously on the road when Isak indicated to Byron that they had found a place to spend the night. Byron agreed, and all the others breathed a sigh of relief. Their stopping place was a large, elongated clearing in the bend of a river. A number of tall trees grew on the bank, forming a natural barrier to the cold air from off the water.

&

Byron stared into the bluish tips of the flames of the fire they had built. Everyone had dined and were now gradually retiring in order to sleep. The two Albanians bedded down right on the trail: one of them slept as the other kept watch. Isak and the Englishmen placed themselves closer to the river. The night was considerably cooler than the day, and the sleeping bodies lay close to the fire. Soon, the only things disturbing the quiet of the night were the murmuring of the river, the light crackling of the fire, and gentle snores. Byron and Isak were the only ones still awake, but neither talked. They lay not too far from one another, and each noticed from his neighbor's breathing that he was not yet asleep. Isak sat up abruptly.

'Sleep won't come to me, my lord,' he said, barely loud enough to be heard. 'I'm going to take a walk.'

Byron stood up in a flash. 'I'm coming too,' he said.

Isak went over to the Albanian keeping watch and whispered something, and then he came back to Byron.

'Let's walk along the river,' he said. 'We were in the saddle for the whole day, and maybe walking a little now will make it easier to sleep.'

They walked along slowly and without a word. The ground beneath their feet was hard, and the thin autumn grass was already wilted and yellowed. The light from the moon was lush and force-ful; it seemed to get caught in the tree branches, already nearly bare and in the eddies of the river. Still they continued to walk side by side. Byron turned his head every few minutes and looked into Isak's pensive face. Isak, his brow furrowed, was biting his lower lip. Once, just as Byron was looking at him, a leaf detached itself from a nearby tree. Reflexively, Isak tried to catch it, but it slid through his fingers.

'Like silk,' Byron said.

'Like Zuleiha,' Isak said.

So Isak's thinking about her too, Byron thought to himself, and for a moment he could not help but think about the girl from Sintra. But immediately a spasm travelled through the fibres of his body: Zuleiha! He asked Isak if he had seen her in the past few days.

'No, my lord,' Isak replied, 'her name has not been uttered since the wedding. All those who'd been saying she would definitely appear are now as silent as can be. Such a story, however, cannot be invented. She is here somewhere, my lord; I can feel it; and I fear that we Iliad will miss her, that she will come to Yannina, and leave again, while I'm away.'

Byron interrupted: 'I cannot comprehend this Eastern predilection for mystification.'

Isak understood not a whit of this, but Byron went on: 'I do not understand all this secretiveness about where she might be. These stories – she's here somewhere, but no one knows exactly where, but then again no one even knows why she would be here.'

'What can a person ever know?' Isak rejoined, 'of what can he be completely certain? People here are careful, my lord, because there's safety in silence. The seductiveness of conversation gives none of us any peace, perhaps for that exact reason. In any case, people here are garrulous despite their caution; they simply say little with their many words. Less frequently, far less frequently, the opposite turns out to be true: that they say a great deal with few words. But those are the conversations which one understands from the very beginning, and they are not typical.' At this point Isak paused briefly. He looked at Byron and went on: 'like our talks, my lord.'

The two men stopped. They had walked too far, and the fire from their campsite was no longer visible.

'We should go back,' Byron said, and Isak turned around without a word. In silence they returned, and the two of them lay down and quickly fell asleep.

CHAPTER SEVEN

October 12, 1809

At dawn the grass was wet. Byron thought that it must have rained. The sky, however, was clear and the air was chilly, and he realized slowly that it must be dew. The two Albanians were sitting by the fire, drinking coffee and smoking. Byron, still supine, looked around. Everyone else was still asleep, except for Isak, who was nowhere to be seen. Byron nearly panicked at the thought that perhaps Isak had made his way back to Yannina already, on account of Zuleiha. Scarcely a moment later, though, he saw him coming back to the camp from the trees along the river. He was adjusting his trousers, and Byron understood what he must have been doing. Meanwhile, he felt the pressure in his own bladder. After Isak had joined the two men at the fire, Byron got to his feet and staggered drowsily over to the trees. His urine coloured the sparse, dewy grass dark yellow, like stale chamomile tea. He went back to join his freshly awakened entourage. Everyone was moving now: Isak was sitting alone at the fire drinking coffee, the Englishmen were slowly rising and stretching their limbs, and the two Albanians had gone over to the horses to untie them. Byron sat down next to Isak, who poured him some coffee.

'Did you sleep well, my lord?'

'Very well. Thanks for asking,' Byron replied.

Soon Hobhouse joined them, and all three began hastily eating their breakfast.

'Yesterday,' Isak said, 'we lost a whole morning, so it's best if we get started as quickly as possible. Also, the route now awaiting us is more difficult than yesterday's.'

And so they rode along for several hours, amidst desultory chatter, until the ascent began. At first it was barely perceptible, but the road turned quickly into a steep and twisting trail. This was no longer the kind of riding that one enjoys. The horses climbed slowly and carefully, and the horsemen had to stay focused every second. They were now moving along in a column, one behind the other, in complete silence. To their left rose the tall, sheer face of the mountain while to the right gaped an ever-deeper abyss. Byron didn't like high places. He was pointedly afraid of them, but he could not stop his eyes from roaming again and again to the right. He couldn't look at the back of Isak's head or at the tail of his horse, which looked like a torn banner; or at the perpendicular white-brown side of the mountain.

The path twisted around like the snake curled around the staff of Asclepius, and Byron's head was swimming from the view into the abyss and the innumerable turns. And he again felt hungry. The ragged sunshine appeared to have dazed him. It was impossible, however, to make a stop: nowhere was there a wide spot, a flat stretch of road, big enough for the men and the animals to catch their breath. They had already been riding for hours. From the position of the sun, Byron knew that it was long past noon. He understood that the horses must also be tired, but it seemed as if they had reconciled themselves to the lack of rest. Eastern fatalism in an animal's way, Byron thought; even in horses here you can see how greatly this country differs from England. As he was reflecting on this, he came face to face with a large curve in the road, beyond which arose the prospect of a nearly vertical ascent.

Now the path grew wider and had no more twists and turns. Byron caught up to Isak, who told him: 'Just this climb now, my lord, and then we will rest up at the top.'

Ten minutes later a large plateau came into view. The squadron of riders stopped, although no one dismounted right away. One of the Albanians said something to Isak, who turned to face Byron.

'It would be best, my lord, if we rested but briefly. If we hurry, we can make it to a village by nightfall, where we can spend a night fit for human beings.'

Byron exchanged brief glances with Hobhouse and then he agreed. He let himself slide off his horse and dropped into the grass.

After several more hours of riding across level ground, the first traces of human habitation became apparent. First they came upon a herd of sheep; a whole sea of dirty white animals sweeping over the meadows on both sides of the road. The old shepherd, wearing a long fur coat, sat peacefully under an isolated tree. Byron looked at him with great curiosity, but the shepherd looked about disinterestedly, as if he saw at least five such groups of mounted men every day.

'Nothing comes as a surprise to the people around here,' said Isak, as though he were reading Byron's thoughts. 'To put it better: there are things that surprise them, but they never show it. Not to be amazed by anything,' Isak continued 'is the best prescription for how to live and survive here.'

Byron mumbled something unintelligible. He was thinking that it was in this corner of the globe that philosophy had been born from that selfsame sense of amazement. Perhaps that is the natural sequence, from initial wonder to resignation and fatalism, Byron thought; just like in human life. If a child were sitting there in the place of that old shepherd, he would have been full of wonder and curiosity, as the orb of the sun crawled slowly but inexorably towards the west.

Soon thereafter they encountered two priests in long black cowls, mounted on small mountain horses. As they neared the band of riders, they moved over to the very edge of the road and passed by with their heads lowered.

'Orthodox priests,' Isak explained, 'Serbian monks, my lord. In the village where we will be spending the night, there is a large monastery.'

'Why are they so submissive?' Byron wanted to know.

'Their religion demands it,' Isak answered with a sarcastic laugh. 'You should know as much, my lord. Here it's wise to bow, or stand aside, and it's even wiser to do both at the same time. Here people don't hold sanctimonious folk of their own faith in very high regard, much less if they are from another religion. But at least the priests in these parts are hospitable, and they are also not poor. They'll take good care of us,' Isak concluded, 'and we'll be able to eat and sleep in their building.'

Byron wondered how much of this was hospitality and how much was pure fear. He was not feeling especially chatty on this late afternoon that was melting away into dusk. The moon was already visible in the dark blue sky, although the sun had not completely set, when they saw the first scattered houses of the mountain village.

'What's the name of this place?' asked Byron.

'Zitza,' Isak responded tersely.

They rode along the dirty village road for a good ten minutes and then caught sight of the outlines of the monastery on the far side of the village. The building, of rustic beauty, was large. Built of hard white stone, and surrounded by a high grey wall, it looked, in the purple half-darkness of impending night, both secretive and warm at the same time. Soon Byron saw the open gate, and at the exact moment that they passed it, the bells boomed forth atmospherically. When they dismounted, the bells stopped as if on command, and a reverberating echo blended with the call of an owl. The wind alternately hid the moon behind the clouds and set it free. It all left a spooky impression, and Byron felt his skin crawling.

'Eastern Gothic, my lord,' whispered Isak, who appeared unnoticed at Byron's side.

From the direction of the main building an old priest made his way towards them, accompanied by two errand-boys. The priest addressed Isak, who in turn translated everything for Byron: 'Fr. Maximilian bids us welcome.'

The two boys led their horses over to the stalls, and Isak, Hobhouse, Byron, and their retinue followed the priest to the main monastery.

The dining hall was a narrow, elongated room with a high ceiling, and immediately upon entering the refectory they were served very hot bowls of soup. A great many candles had been lit, but the flames gave off only a sickly yellow glow. In the middle of the room stood a long, rectangular table at which approximately twenty priests were seated; with the guests taking their places at the end of the table nearest the door. By sheer chance, Byron ended up sitting across from the Abbot of the monastery, Fr. Maximilian. No one broke the silence, and the soup was quickly consumed. Then fish was brought out, river trout with red dots on its smooth, silvery skin, and with soft off-white flesh and delicate bones. The morsels turned into pure poetry in Byron's mouth. He told Isak that never before had he eaten such a delicious fish, and his words were translated to the Abbot, who in turn mumbled an answer while chewing contentedly. When the fish had also been consumed, sweets were served: almonds, fruit and sherbet.

'I take it the fish was to your liking, my lord?' inquired Isak.

'It was the finest I've ever eaten.'

'Fish like this are only to be found here,' Isak continued with an air of mystery, 'and there's also a story about them.'

'A story?' Byron looked at him quizzically. What kind of story?'

Isak seemed to have been waiting for that question: 'A long, very very long, time ago, my lord, before the Normans set sail from your island homeland, Byzantium ruled this entire country. This empire was not so different from today's Ottoman Empire; they both had the same capital city, and, for the most part, the same territories. The difference was that the Byzantine emperor's realm was not yet illuminated by the light of Islam. Instead, it was ruled by the religion in whose retreat we dined so deliciously this evening. And in the same way that some local notable or other is constantly rising up against the Sultan nowadays, people rebelled against the Byzantine Emperor back then. One of these strong mutineers, powerful but fly-by-night, and if I may be so bold...' and at this point Isak's voice trailed off to a whisper '...a contemporary Ali Pasha,' and now his voice returned to its earlier volume '...was named Samuel. At least that's how you Englishmen would call him. "God has heard me," such is the meaning of this name. This Samuel wanted to be no more and no less than the Macedonian Alexander the Great. And one must admit that he started out rather well. He shook the throne of the Emperor and declared himself to be the ruler. The years went by and he ruled uncontested, but the power went to his head. In a decisive battle he tried his luck against the Emperor, but he was defeated, and his entire army was taken prisoner. Samuel himself was able to escape. Now hear me out, my lord. Listen to what the Emperor did to the prisoners, of whom there were thousands. He blinded them, all of them, my lord; he had their eyes gouged out.'

Byron stared at him in shock.

'No, my lord, not every one of them, actually. To be precise, he left every hundredth man with one eye. Every hundredth, my lord, so that the column of blinded men could find its way back to its commander. Imagine this procession, my lord: thousands upon thousands of blind men, led by a handful of lucky one-eyed wretches. When Samuel saw them, his heart burst: but not immediately. He first sat down on the shore of a lake and shed bloody tears. It's from his tears that the fish here got their red dots, and because of his tears their flesh is so tender.'

Having related this, Isak fell silent, but Byron continued looking at him, spellbound. 'What a story,' he said at last.

'Every child here, my lord, knows it. Samuel exists in the Byzantine chronicles, and the story of the ravaged eyes is also historically attested; after all, the part with the bloody eyes is not so hard to believe.'

'This story of sitting on the shore reminds me of something,' Byron mused.

Isak smiled. 'I know, my lord. Let me help you. It reminds you of Aegeus, the father of Theseus, and the black sails.'

Byron slapped his palm to his forehead: Yes, that was it!

'It's the same world, my lord. Then, as now, we live the mythology.'

Their conversation was interrupted by someone clearing his throat. Byron raised his eyes and saw the priests slowly getting up from the table.

'The evening meal is ended, my lord, our hosts will retire now, and we will also be led to our quarters. Sleep soundly, for tomorrow brings more riding.'

CHAPTER EIGHT

October 13, 1809

It rained the entire night. Byron slept well, waking only a couple of times in the course of the evening to the sound of raindrops. There was no storm or downpour, the wind was not whipping about, and no thunder or lightning split the heavens; it was simply a strong rain; constant, not heavy and not light. The morning nonetheless proved to be dry. The sky was grey, the ground wet, the horizon foggy, but there was no more precipitation. When Byron awoke, he opened the window. A keen, pleasant cool breeze forced its way into the room, tainted with an aromatic wisp of garlic, the way it often is after a rain. Byron noted with satisfaction that they had avoided the downpour in the most fortuitous way possible, and he envisaged that the riding today would be pleasant. He was agreeably hungry and looking forward to a feast of a breakfast; he was in a good mood as he walked to the dining room. People had already set to eating with vigour, and Byron was happy to join them. The priests and the Englishmen were in fine fettle; the two Albanians gave, as ever, the impression of indifference; only Isak gave off a worried air.

'We slept through the rain – isn't that perfect?' Byron said to him.

'I would be happy, my lord, if you prove to be right about that, but I have my doubts,' Isak responded distractedly.

After breakfast the Abbot uttered a few sentences, and Isak nodded in agreement.

'What did he say?' Byron wanted to know.

Isak grinned cynically: 'He is offering their hospitality for as long as we might want it, although yesterday I told him that we are in a hurry to move on. Nothing is sweeter than parading hospitality that you know will be declined.'

'That's a shame,' Byron responded. 'I find the monastery interesting. I'd like to stay here a while, get a better look at it. Wander through the library and chat with the priests.' 'Maybe on the return journey, my lord,' answered Isak. 'You have to return to Yannina anyway, before you travel on to Athens and Istanbul. But for now it's best if we move as fast as we can. Believe me, my lord, I'd love it if I were wrong about this, but in a short while there is going to come a rain the likes of which you have never seen.'

Byron shook his head in disbelief. But at any rate he was aware that Isak was right about the return journey. He would by necessity come the same way again, and would then visit the monastery for a while longer. There was no need to delay things now; it would be best to put in an appearance in front of Ali Pasha as soon as possible.

'Then let's make a move,' he said to Isak.

They left the building and the boys brought them their mounts. The horses had also been rested, fed, and groomed. Byron swung his leg over his black steed and patted its mane. The gate to the compound was opened, and the little troop set off into the late morning grey of an autumn day, to the accompaniment of ringing of bells.

It was probably due to a command from Isak that the Albanians moved at a furious tempo. Was it on account of their speed, the jovial mood, or the actual beauty of the landscape that led Byron to believe he had never laid eyes on lovelier views in this part of the world than here? Billows of fog, thick like foam, floated around the majestic mountain peaks like angels; the trees with their bare profiles of densely interwoven branches reminded him of shaggy paintbrushes with residual spots of paint; the diaphanous vapour rising from the river mixed with the creamy white ejaculate of the rapids. In the chiaroscuro of the gloomy mid-day, everything white gave the impression of something other-worldly. Byron enjoyed the landscape without having the desire to slow down or stop. It was the kind of beauty that hides its most profound essence behind the fact that one experiences it in leisurely, random doses; it is an unobtrusive beauty that doesn't change your life yet also cannot be ignored. A permanent smile hovered on Byron's face.

It seemed that no one else seemed to take as much pleasure in the journey. The two Albanians at whose backs he was staring rode along swiftly and easily, but mechanically. It took all of Hobhouse's effort to keep pace with Byron and Isak, who looked genuinely worried. From time to time he inspected the sky, and although Byron thought that nothing had changed for the better or the worse, Isak obviously was of a different opinion. He mumbled, as if to himself: 'maybe we should have stayed with the priests.' It crossed Byron's mind that Isak might be carrying on a bit theatrically: he appeared to be enjoying the role of sage, in cahoots with the mysteries of nature. Because at this moment, if they should for some reason require a drop of rain, there wouldn't even be enough to take one's medicine.

Byron, accustomed to the English climate, to those frequent afternoons when the rain stops suddenly, suddenly and briefly, and then starts right up again, on and on for eternity – Byron truly liked an autumn like this. Here it rained fairly hard for a couple of hours, and then it stopped, and that was it. There weren't these boring stretches of drizzle, which looked innocuous but which in the long run left a person more soaked through than did the strongest shower; there was no constant dripping, like a curtain on the world; there was none of that cold, windy, diagonally plunging rain. It was simply thus: either it was raining, or it wasn't. And at the moment, it was not raining; not a single drop had fallen on his cheek, the back of his hand, or the horse's head.

All this time Isak kept his eyes riveted on the sky, and he mumbled something under his breath. He seems displeased that it isn't raining, Byron thought; and if the burst of rain doesn't come down for five more days, he'll still say it's exactly what he predicted. With a perverse sense of satisfaction, Byron stared at Isak every time he looked up. Meanwhile, Isak did not react to any of this; but he did call out, after every one of his numerous glances up at the heavens, something to the two men riding along in front of them, and they then spurred their horses on to a gallop. Byron was just about to say something, when the bottom fell out of the sky. He could not have imagined that a rain such as that could fall; as if it were not a rain consisting of drops, but a gigantic torrent cascading down from the sky, like a waterfall, like wine decanted. At first Byron didn't consider this rain to be either an inconvenience or a danger; he cast his eyes about as if bewitched. It was raining so hard that even the summits of the mountains in the distance could not be seen clearly. Instead, he felt like a diver looking at an underwater reef, rising up from the floor of the sea. The silhouettes of the riders next to him were also blurry. Isak shouted something, but Byron couldn't understand him. Finally he caught enough to know that in the vicinity somewhere was a cave.

They followed the two Albanians as they turned off the main route. The hooves of the horses sank into the muddy path, and the raindrops struck the ground with such force that the riders were spattered with dirt from underneath. Byron remembered just then that the rain had commenced when there was no sign yet of dusk, but now the clouds hung so low, and it was so dark, that the day was indistinguishable from the night. Soon lightning began, and the world lit up from one second to the next with an unreal shine; while thunder echoed like a cannonade. The horses reared up in fright more and more often. Fletcher, one of the Englishmen in Byron's entourage, tumbled off his horse, but fortunately he sustained no injury. Isak leapt down from his mount to see what kind of help he should offer, and then climbed back into the saddle. The others paused and waited for them. At precisely that moment more lightning flashed, and Hobhouse caught sight of the entrance to the cave. As the echo of thunder rolled over the earth, the dripping horses and men made for the grotto. In the soaked earth the animals left hoof-prints as if they were walking on snow or sand.

§

The cave was as spacious and comfortable as a cave could be. It was split into two more or less equally large sections. The first part was approximately ten metres long, ten metres wide, and four to five metres high. Beyond it the floor dropped half a metre, forming a broad step, and then the cave continued beyond. This second section was somewhat deeper, but its natural ceiling grew gradually lower until it was barely one metre high. The group made their way into the back section, while the horses remained up front, in the antechamber, as Byron termed it. Soon they had all warmed themselves at a freshly kindled fire. The men placed it between themselves and the horses, at the base of the step, so they could share the heat and some of the smoke could make its way outside. A simple supper, without table, chairs, or eating utensils, was soon behind them.

Immediately after the meal, everyone save Isak and Byron lay down to rest. Isak stared meditatively at the wall of the cave; Byron busied himself with the fire, adding a big tree stump now and again, so that it would smoulder until morning. As the fire crackled anew, an unclear word that Isak had whispered caught Byron's ear. What kind of plateau? Byron wondered. Did Isak mean the low flat platform in the interior of their cave, or did he mean the high plain across which they were travelling? Byron looked inquisitively at Isak, who added: 'The parable of the cave.'

In a fraction of a second Byron realized that Isak wasn't talking about a plateau but rather about Plato. On the wall, the horses' shadows were clearly outlined. Byron grinned and caught Isak's eye. Isak smiled back at him. There was something magical about the fact that two men, at midnight in a cave, with the Great Flood raging outside, would both call to mind a classical philosopher and a story he had written more than two millennia ago. This time there's no need to tell each other stories, Byron thought; a single word had been enough to know that we're both familiar with this story and are both thinking the same thing.

The first snores were now coming from their companions and from outside came the swooshing of falling water and the muffled reverberations of thunder; the two men remained silent and let their thoughts wander to Plato. This was, after all, more or less the territory, the region, from which Plato hailed, and it was because of Plato that Byron had set out for this part of the world. For Plato was a metaphor for Hellas, for the *Iliad* and the *Odyssey*, for Chapman's *Homer*, for Achilles and Patrocles, and Hector and Paris and Priam, for Zeno and the turtle, Aristotle and Socrates, Zeus, Hera, Apollo, Athena, Dionysius, Ares, and Aphrodite. Plato was the metaphor for everything upon which his culture and identity was based. From Plato were descended Virgil and the Gospels according to John and St. Augustine. The concept of love on which Byron's life rested was in turn derived from Plato. Without Plato, there would not be a Mary Anne Chaworth, and actually no Marias anywhere; nor would there be any Sintra or any girl from Sintra, no Helen of Troy and no Zuleiha. 'A metaphor,' Byron whispered. Now Isak was looking at him, but the expression on his face was puzzling.

'Soon,' he said, 'you'll be travelling on to Athens, right, my lord?' Byron nodded his head.

'Do you know how the Greeks use the word metaphor?' Isak asked.

'The same way we do,' Byron shot back. 'As a symbol.'

Isak laughed out loud, so loudly in fact that Hobhouse jolted out of his sleep. 'No, my lord, there you are wrong. For the Greeks, a metaphor is the same as it was thousands of years ago,' Isak said through his chuckle. 'When you need a carriage in Athens, call for a "metaphor," and you will be presented with a quite tangible carriage with horses and a driver, and not with Apollo's team or a bridled Pegasus. In Greek, "metaphor" is still the word for a conveyance. It is still true to its etymology, without any Western literary associations.'

'Are you being serious?' Byron asked.

'Very serious, my lord,' Isak confirmed. 'But that's the Balkans for you: here Plato is still alive in the caves, and a metaphor is not made of paper but of solid wood and living flesh. Let's turn in, my lord, but with the way this rain is coming down, you should not be surprised if we don't wake up for three hundred years.'

With that Isak turned towards the fire and lay down. Judging from his breath, he fell asleep forthwith. Byron was left alone for a long time with the shadows of the horses, before he too drifted off to sleep.

CHAPTER NINE

October 14, 1809

Byron was awakened by the feeling that someone was looking at him. He opened his eyes to find Isak's gaze on him.

'Good morning,' Isak said.

He was evidently the first one out of bed; for everyone else was still asleep. Meanwhile, as if on command, the others began to stir. It was still raining, Isak proclaimed to all; no longer so violently, but still fairly heavily.

'So the weather is moderating,' Byron murmured.

Isak replied that he wouldn't quite say that. 'This is more of a short respite. That's why we should get moving quickly, if we don't intend to spend several more days in this cave. If we head out now and don't pause to rest, we can, by my calculation, reach a *han* by nightfall,' Isak concluded.

His eyes scanned the room. The Albanians nodded hastily, while Byron and Hobhouse shrugged their shoulders. Hobhouse walked over to the entrance of the cave, and he came back a few seconds later: 'It's still raining ferociously. We should wait a few more hours, or at least eat something first,' he said, turning to face Isak.

'No,' Isak said, 'that's not possible. We have to make use of the day and its light. It's going to rain even harder, believe me.'

So with collars up and heads covered by caps and scarves, they all led their horses out of the cave, spurred them on, and rode off. The rain continued its intense drumming on the earth, but the thunder and wind had ceased. All around them lay evidence of nature's fury from the night before. There were broken boughs and branches everywhere, and many smaller trees had been completely ripped out of the ground; the earth was plowed up, and the road was strewn with numerous puddles and swamp-like pools. The stubborn rain drew fleeting concentric circles on the surface of these shallow but turbid waters. Byron, riding along with his head down, watched intently as the puddles were bombarded by droplets and sent up dirty, cold spurts of water in response. They soon reached the highway, which had not been spared by the storm. The river had overflowed its banks at one point, and they literally had to ride through water for several hundred metres.

'It's a good thing that we got an early start,' Isak said to Hobhouse, 'because by this afternoon it will be a great deal more difficult to get through here, and by tomorrow it might well be impossible. We would have to make a long detour around this whole area, and it would then have taken fifteen days to get to Tepelena.'

Gradually the rain again poured down harder and harder. The road was deserted: since they broke camp that morning, they had not encountered a single living creature. Now, though, Byron caught sight of a massive silhouette in the sky. An eagle, giant and solitary, flew over them. Isak looked up as well, and said: 'That is a terrifying bird. It's the wolf among birds. It attacks snipes but does not spare even lambs. Do you know, my lord, how Aeschylus died?'

Byron shook his head in the negative.

'Eagles like that take hold of tortoises and smash their armour by dropping them onto rocks from high in the air. They say that an eagle mistook Aeschylus' bald, pale head for a stone and subsequently smashed it with a tortoise, so that human brains and the meat of the animal were mixed together.'

Byron shuddered. Zeno's paradox about Achilles and the tortoise occurred to him: as great as the distance was between the elegant and sophisticated mathematical problem and the rustic tale, superficially they had much in common. They linked the names of writings from the classical world with a large, unthreatening, long-lived animal. The myths were alive here in the Balkans, just as Isak had declared the day before. Then, just as their small squad was coming out of a curve in the road, Byron heard one of the Albanians shout. In front of them stood an enormous tree, a remarkably tall and thick oak, perhaps thousands of years old. Isak was surprised, but he was also pleased.

'We're almost there!' he called out. He turned to face Byron and Hobhouse: 'We are closer to the *han* than I thought. We'll be there, I believe, in less than an hour.'

Everyone breathed a sigh of relief, despite the increasingly heavy rain. It was only a short time until the outlines of the *han* were discernible on the horizon. The horses broke into a gallop, as if they, too, were overjoyed.

The *han* was a hive of activity. A sum of money and the mention of Ali Pasha's name ensured that Byron and the others quickly obtained good rooms. Isak merely had to utter two or three sentences to the innkeeper and everything was settled. The arrival of this unusual company of people did arouse some curiosity though; the men who sat smoking and playing cards in the forecourt of the *han* looked up at them and started to whisper. These idlers and brigands, with their tattered tunics and bloodshot eyes, did not exactly make a peaceable impression. Byron watched them out of the corner of his eye, cautiously, so that their gazes did not meet, and he also avoided turning his back to them. Isak said under his breath: 'Have no fear, my lord. It is written on your brow, so to speak, that you are under the protection of Ali Pasha. Believe me, no one will so much as look askance at you, believe me.'

'Who are those people then?'

'Who knows, my lord, who knows…. Some of them are just passing through and have taken shelter from the rain, as we have done; others however are cut-throats and robbers of the type who always hang around places like this. They would like nothing better than to deprive a person of his worldly possessions, my lord,' Isak went on, 'but whoever has a real fortune need not fear them at all, because in the end they will all kill each other.'

'Let everyone go now to his own room!' Isak said at last, to their whole group. 'Rest your bodies and souls.'

'How long will we be staying here?' asked Hobhouse, who had overheard the brief conversation between Byron and Isak.

'Until the storm is finished,' Isak answered. 'In two nights, perhaps three, the rains will be over.'

At these words they parted, each looking for his room. It turned out that Isak and Byron were sharing a room, and Hobhouse took one with Fletcher and Collins; with the other Englishmen ending up in a third room, with the two Albanians in a fourth. The room for Isak and Byron was somewhat larger than the others, and was fitted-out with two hard wooden bunks at either end, and a large, roughly hewn table in the middle. There were no chairs. Directly upon entering, Byron dropped onto a bed, while Isak continued to pace back and forth. The noisy rain went on undiminished. Byron rolled over to face the wall, but he could tell, by the heavy footfalls, that Isak was still pacing about the room. He did so nervously, with rapid, loud steps. Byron sat up suddenly. Isak paused and said, 'Forgive me, my lord. Were you trying to sleep?'

'Actually I wasn't, if I were to lie back down now, I definitely wouldn't sleep a wink tonight. The problem is that when I am faced with a choice between sitting and lying down, I naturally prefer to lie down, and in a room without chairs of course I recline.' 'That's interesting,' Isak said tentatively. 'Here in the East, sitting and lying are not such strictly differentiated positions. People here somehow prefer to be half-sitting or half-lying, whether it's on benches, mattresses, or pillows.' He paused for a moment and then continued, 'it probably has something to do with hard and soft. The West is hard and the East is soft, or is that too much of a generalization?'

'I have already noticed this penchant for categorization, as I would put it in Oriental terms,' Byron asserted with a laugh. 'But here the issue isn't sitting or lying, but rather walking.'

'So the noise did disturb you,' Isak said more earnestly. 'I was of the opinion that you didn't intend to sleep.'

'No, It did not bother me and I was not trying to sleep. I am simply not used to seeing a person walk back and forth continually in a room, as if it were a prison cell.'

Now it was Isak's turn to laugh. 'As far as I'm concerned, my lord,' he said, 'it's like this: if I am not doing anything, or when I'm not speaking to anyone, I can neither stand nor sit, and if I am not sleeping, I cannot lie down either. I have to walk, and it's how I best think over things. It does not matter if I am in the field or in a run-down hut.'

' So you are a Peripatetic, 'Byron said, with kindness and a touch of disguised irony.

Isak fired back: 'A lonely, laconic, pathetic Peripatetic. But for now, if you really aren't going to sleep, we could go down and have a bite, for I am starving.'

Isak continued behaving strangely, or at least it appeared thus to Byron. At the meal, his mind seemed elsewhere. Byron asked a question, about some completely trivial matter, but Isak did not appear to have heard him at all. He ate slowly and half-heartedly, although a little earlier he'd complained of hunger. Byron wondered if he was becoming ill. He looked a little more closely at him, as if he were searching for symptoms. But nothing in Isak's face indicated illness or frailty. *"I guess the man is just in a bit of a bad mood, or maybe he's feeling down on account of all the rain,"* Byron concluded. Just then he noticed Hobhouse, who had apparently just come down to eat. He beckoned to him, and as Hobhouse joined them at the table, it was as if Isak had been waiting for this opportunity. Standing up, he said he was going to take a short walk.

'It's still raining,' Byron responded.

'I know,' Isak said curtly.

Byron and Hobhouse watched him leave.

'What's wrong with him?' Hobhouse asked. Byron shrugged his shoulders. Without Isak, he felt somewhat ill at ease in the *han*, left to the mercy of the other guests. He was not afraid, but it irked him that without Isak he was a man without ears or tongue. Thus he might mistake a greeting for a threat, or a threat for a greeting, and he wouldn't be able to do so much as ask for water. Hobhouse wolfed down the food he was served. The two of them said nothing to each other the entire time, as if they had silently agreed not to draw unnecessary attention to themselves with unintelligible words as long as they had no one at their side who would fend off possible intruders in their own language. Byron was also aware of the fact that people were staring at them intently, and he sensed a special abhorrence in their glances. Ali Pasha's name had drawn an invisible line around them and now it protected them the way a heavy cloak protects you from the rain. After they had emptied the bowls in front of them, Byron and Hobhouse sat on for a bit in silence. Dusk was falling, and the front-court of the inn gradually emptied. Soon the two Englishmen retired to their rooms.

But Byron wasn't tired. He lit a candle, and shortly thereafter he found himself doing what Isak had been doing – walking up and down the room. *"Now all that's missing is for me to go out for a stroll in the rain,"* he thought, and at that very moment the door opened. Isak had returned, and he wasn't even particularly wet.

'Is it still coming down?' Byron asked, just to have something to say; the muffled noise from outside was supplying a clear answer.

'Yes,' Isak replied, 'it's still raining, and heavily at that.' He sat down on his bed.

'That means that tonight nothing will come of your peripatetic ambling,' Byron spluttered with a laugh.

Isak did not seem to have understood.

'That pacing back and forth in the room,' Byron explained, 'I tried it too. Not such a bad idea.'

Isak was in a visibly bad mood. He nodded his head, commented that he was tired, and stretched out on his bed. Byron, from his own bed, saw Isak lying on his back, but there was no way of knowing whether he was asleep or just staring at the ceiling.

'The best place to look is always at the ceiling, the blue-blooded lady said' Byron whispered, thinking that he might be merely talking to himself.

The chuckle from the other side of the room revealed that Isak was awake.

'Such bits of popular wisdom, my lord, are to be found in both the East and the West, among noblewomen and beggars; at least we are no different in this regard. People here say that a woman's life is hell by day and paradise by night,' Isak went on.

Byron called to mind Teiresias, the only person ever to have been both man and woman in his lifetime, and he recalled the wager between Hera and Zeus. 'Teiresias,' he began--but there was no response. *"He's probably drifted off,"* Byron thought, getting up for a moment to put out the candle. For a long time Byron lay in the dark and stared out into the impenetrable blackness. As slumber at last descended and his eyelids closed, he thought he heard Isak get quietly of bed, open the door, and leave the room. Maybe I'm dreaming, Byron thought. And with that, he sank into Morpheus' arms.

CHAPTER TEN

October 15, 1809

When Byron woke up, Isak wasn't there. Indeed, he had apparently run off somewhere in the wee hours. It occurred to Byron that perhaps he didn't go anywhere till this morning, and he had dreamt the rest. But in fact he knew he was just trying to find comfort in such thoughts. He was at present more dependent upon Isak that he wanted to admit to himself. And to think that he actually knew nothing about him, despite their regular conversations and mutual avowals. He had read or heard somewhere that people from the Orient, the Balkans, and the Levant are sometimes, at irregular intervals, overcome by a type of shiftlessness, a kind of periodic madness, so that they disappear from their dwellings and frequent obscure taverns, drinking and carrying on until at some later point they return to their homes, peaceful and well-behaved, shy and docile. "*Social epilepsy, or something like that,*" thought Byron. It seemed to him that Isak had most likely succumbed to something like that.

The rain continued strong and implacable, and Byron assumed that Isak couldn't have gone far. That comforted him somehow in the midst of this whole situation. There soon came a knock at the door, and he opened it cautiously. It was Hobhouse.

'Still raining,' he said, 'are you hungry?'

'Let's go down,' Byron suggested.

'Where's Isak?'

'I don't know,' Byron shot back.

Downstairs, at the large table, their whole little caravan was sitting down to eat; everyone except Isak. Byron and Hobhouse joined them. The two Albanian escorts had no idea where Isak was, or at least that's how Byron interpreted their mutely inquisitive glances. Immediately after the meal, Byron withdrew to his room. The *han* struck him as dreary and empty. The rain was having a depressive effect on him, too. Listlessly, he stretched out on his bed. He had barely been awake for an hour but would've liked nothing better than to go back to sleep. He had a couple of books with him, but had no desire to read. Suddenly he had an inspiration: he stood up and pulled the large table over to his bed, and then he fetched a pen and paper. He would write his mother a letter.

🙷

Dearest Mother,

I've been in Turkey for some time now. Four weeks ago we set out in a warship from Malta, and we arrived, after ten days at sea, in the Turkish Mediterranean port of Preveza. We did not remain there long, but headed straight for the mountains. The proper name for this province is Albania. In a few days I am supposed to meet its ruler, Ali Pasha, a man about whom one hears only good things here. Although I have still never laid eyes on him, I can say that he has exhibited extraordinary and rare hospitality to me. Somehow he heard that an Englishman of noble lineage was on his territory, and he commanded his people to take care of my every need; there is no chance of my being allowed to pay for anything.

In the city of Yannina, my entourage and I lodged in a house that had been put at my disposal, and we dined upon the most wonderful foods of the Orient. Now I am *en route* to the city of Tepelena, where Ali Pasha is expecting me. Incidentally, he rules not only over Albania but also over Epirus and Macedonia, and his family also controls Morea and has great influence in Egypt. I have already met Husein Bey and Mahmut Pasha, Ali Pasha's grandsons, in Yannina. Both of them are still young, but they do not remind one in the least of English boys their age. They are already little men. I cannot recall ever having seen more delightful boys. Mahmut Pasha gave me a magnificent Albanian garment: a long white kilt, a gold-embroidered cape, a purple silk jacket with hems of gold stitching, and a jerkin in the same pattern. I have not yet tried them on, but with my silver pistols and my *hançer*, I will truly look like an Albanian. I like Albania, and the Albanians, very much. The Albanians are either Muslims or Christians, but their appearance hardly varies accordingly.

The countryside is beautiful. The section of coastline that I have seen is prettier than anything in Spain or Malta, and the sea at Preveza gleams in such a peculiar way that I cannot tell if its real colour is purplish-blue or bluish-green. The smell of salt from the sea blends with the intoxicating aroma of the pines. The trees growing by the ocean are bent back towards the continent, probably on account of the wind that blows in constantly from the water. Like dogs, they bend down before the hand that feeds them, and their boughs seem to have their doubts as to whether that is the sky or the earth. If you lean against a tree like this, your hand gets sticky with sap as thick as honey.

Just a few miles east of these calm coves along the Mediterranean, however, rise mountains that are harsh but proud. Albania is, truth be told, a mountainous land. The magical attractiveness of these lofty mountains reminded me immediately of Scotland. The whole region has something of the stories and novels of Walter Scott, something noble, solid, and venerable. Narrow paths twist past thick forests, frothing watercourses leap over stones of white flint, and the everlasting snow on the summits caresses the downy cloudlets on the blue canopy. Under the resplendent sun, landscapes of fairy tales and dreams let themselves be discovered, but let just a few clouds push their way in front of the sun, and it's enough to remind one that nowhere is there as much evil as in fairy tales, and that nightmares are dreams, too.

A rain of Biblical proportions descended upon us recently: the tracks are impassable, the streams are swollen, and in the grey, rainy air neither mountain peaks nor sky can be seen. But do not be afraid for me, Mother, for I am safe and am waiting tonight in a pleasant inn for the rain to cease. I believe that I wrote to you from Malta about the virtues of Lady Spencer Smith and my joy at having the good fortune to meet such a person in an unfamiliar land. A similar thing has transpired here.

Ali Pasha has assigned his personal physician to me as interpreter. His name is Isak, and he speaks excellent English. Without him I would be well nigh helpless here, but what is even more important, I believe, is that we have become so intimate that I can count him a friend. His life story is even more interesting than that of Lady Spencer Smith. I would very much like to tell you his story, but I have neither time nor space now. I haven't even managed to tell you aught of the city of Yannina or that village with the Orthodox monastery in which I spent a night, or about the local weddings and a thousand other things.

I will write about all of that, perhaps, in the letters to follow. In general I am doing well, and am in good health, as is my companion, Mr. Hobhouse. And the same is true for all the others in my retinue. A few days ago Fletcher fell off his horse, but fortunately sustained no injuries. I have almost forgotten England in this place, and there is probably nothing from there that it would interest me to hear except that you are well and happy. It would be best for you to write me in care of the English consulate in Athens.

I will also write to you again as soon as I have an opportunity. It is difficult for me to find the time to write, and so you must remember: if my letters do not arrive often, that doesn't mean that all is not well with me, or that I don't want to reach out to you. Please believe me. I love you and am thinking of you.

Your devoted son,
Byron

Byron's day had passed very quickly. The onset of dusk seemed to him to arrive the moment he finished the letter. He had written slowly and deliberately, paying attention to his handwriting and to every word, yet it still astonished him that he had written for almost an entire day. At first he couldn't believe that it was already so late; it was cloudy, and day and dusk overlapped. He was not bothered that another rainy day was behind them, but Isak's continued absence filled him with great concern. With the onset of darkness, truly grim thoughts began to plague Byron. It occurred to him that perhaps someone had taken Isak's life, which made his skin crawl. Yesterday Isak had been flashing a lot of money around with the owner of the *han*, in order to get them the best rooms, and one of the numerous bandits lurking around down there must have seen it. For all of Isak's attempts at explaining in rational terms the behaviour of the local thugs, Byron remained quite aware that such attempts at explanation did not hold water. 'These are bandits, not mathematicians,' Byron said inaudibly to himself, regretting that he had not told Isak this. Instead, he had just wordlessly agreed with his arguments. Byron mused that consequences were almost never on the minds of these people. One hour ahead, at most one day, that is the time frame with which they concern themselves. *Eventual punishments do not bother them,* he thought; *their understanding does not extend that far.*

Byron stood up and began to wander around. His state of mind now fell under the description of "panic." He could imagine Isak's corpse, drenched by the rain and lying in a ditch; he could see clearly the slit throat and many holes in his chest, and his fingers seemed to feel the warmth of Isak's blood. The dead eyes stared into the emptiness, the forehead was damp and cold as ice, and the rain pelted the water, pooling in his half-opened mouth. And although this vision filled Byron with horror, there was something more terrible still. A thought had taken shape in his mind; it was as clear a sentence as a beloved line of poetry or an ancient maxim: If Isak has been killed then there is no salvation for us. For the first time on this long journey Byron felt something akin to fear. He did not fear death, but he was terrorized and humiliated by the thought that his life could be snuffed out by some of these stinking, Balkan knaves. But it lasted only a moment. One look at his pistol and knife replaced the fear inside of him with a renewed will to fight. Some of those degenerates would pay for their impudence before Byron's body hit the ground. Maybe it'd be wise for me to go see Hobhouse so that we can make a plan, he thought; if we stand together, we stand a chance of saving ourselves. We could also continue on our journey despite the rain and darkness, and that would be better than waiting here for our executioners.

At that moment, all of a sudden, someone knocked at his door. Byron's muscles grew taut, like a cat ready to leap. That's not Hobhouse, he thought quickly; his knock is much lighter. Byron picked up his pistol and walked to the door. So this is how it begins, he thought. With his back pressed to the wall, he slowly turned the key without opening the door. For a few seconds all was quiet in the corridor, and then the door opened. Byron's perspiring hand clutched the grip of the pistol. I want to see you before I kill you... And into the room walked Isak. He was not taken aback when he saw Byron, pistol in hand, leaning against the wall. Instead, he tottered into the room and tumbled onto his bed. Surely he's drunk, Byron assumed, but he could detect any stench of alcohol on the man. Isak had left the door open, so Byron closed it and crossed over to Isak's bed. He lay on his back with his eyes closed, but not drunk at all.

'What happened to your key?'

Isak made no answer.

'Where were you?' Still no reply. 'Are things all right?'

Isak neither grunted nor spoke, nor did he open his eyes. He was pressing his eyelids together like a cowed child.

'Fine,' Byron said, as if to himself. 'Fine. So now I get it. This is the place where boys behave like adults, and grown men behave like children.' Meanwhile it seemed that nothing could make Isak utter even one word. A few more times over the course of that evening Byron sought to converse with him, but his words were in vain. At some point, Byron extinguished the light and lay down to sleep. In the pitch-black room, Isak's voice echoed in a ghostly way.

'They're here,' he said.

'Ali Pasha is here?' Byron replied in a sleepy mumble.

'No, Zuleiha,'

And Byron was awake in an instant. But he didn't have time to say a single word.

'Don't ask me any questions, my lord,' Isak protested. 'We'll talk about it tomorrow. I promise.'

CHAPTER ELEVEN

October 16, 1809

Byron had slept well. He woke up feeling rested and cheerful. In the night the rain had sung him a lullaby, while Zuleiha's presence resounded, refrain-like, in his head. Still lying down, Byron looked over at Isak's bed. Isak was lying on his stomach, hugging his pillow. He appeared to be sleeping. Byron did not want to wake him. But he had to move, had to sit up, even though he knew that would make the bed creak. Some kind of energy was bubbling up within him. Energy – that everlasting joy, as someone had once said – although Byron could not remember at the moment who that was. The rain gave signs of slackening, even if only gradually. It continued to fall steadily, but the horizon was no longer so grey. The light spilling across the room was no longer as subdued; it contained minute traces of sun, like a river flowing with gold. The light must also have awakened Isak, for a moment later he turned over on his side, rubbed his eyes, and opened them. His gaze met Byron's immediately, and he furrowed his brow in puzzlement upon noticing his room-mate's euphoric mood. But Isak had been much restored by his sleep, as well. There were no more traces of yesterday's confusion and exhaustion, of the silence and secrecy. He stood up quickly, and, as was his wont, began to pace back and forth.

'Last night it took me a long time to go to sleep, my lord, in contrast to you. I was wound up like a top, and I talked and talked and wondered why you didn't answer, but you were asleep. I talked and talked, like seldom before in my life, so perhaps it's actually better that you didn't hear it. I talked for so long that it must have finally worn me out, and I fell asleep. I had great need of a proper sleep.' Isak blurted all of this out as he moved about, and then he sat down on the edge of the bed. He looked at Byron. A smile hovered on the Englishman's face.

'What was the subject of this nocturnal monologue directed at a sleeping man?'

'It was about Zuleiha, my lord. Only I'm thinking that the monologue wasn't for you; I was talking for my own benefit. It was necessary for me to find the words for everything that had built up inside me. To me it seems the more important conversation is with myself, even when my counterpart is asleep,' Isak continued. 'Poets know this quite well, because, while a poem is, for convention's sake, addressed to a listener, its essence lies in what the poet is saying to himself.'

Isak stopped talking; Byron thought of Marcus Aurelius.

'I saw her, my lord,' Isak said after a short silence.

Byron said nothing. He vowed to himself: don't interrupt him, don't ask him anything, let him say it all himself. Isak paused again, looking past Byron at the wall, but soon his words began to flow rapidly.

'Shortly behind us, my lord, a large caravan from Bosnia came in. Wealthy and respected people, I could tell, because the owner of the *han* took them in as if they were his own kith and kin. They arrived from the opposite direction: they are headed to Yannina, and after that Istanbul. I heard the way the innkeeper turned to the leader of the caravan and called him Selim Beg. From somewhere in Bosnia that name was familiar to me, but at first it didn't ring a bell. I spent the whole afternoon mulling it over, my lord, after we had taken our lodgings here. Then, my lord, in the evening I heard someone singing in Bosnian – beautifully, slowly and effortlessly. And then it all clicked in my head. Of Zuleiha's brother, Selim, it is said that he is a lovely singer. People were saying that at the wedding of Zaim Aga's son. 'You are going to hear a proper song when Selim

Beg gets here,' they said. That means that Zuleiha must have also been in the caravan, I thought, but surely they are going to keep her hidden. I made an effort to strike up a conversation with several of the Bosnians, about topics like the rain and the condition of the road, but they all made a point of avoiding contact. Fine, Bosnians are known for being cautious, and acting arrogantly, and I knew that this need not be anything out of the ordinary. But something in my gut told me that Zuleiha was there; somehow my nose was twitching at the prospect; I sniffed it out, the way a dog finds its master. And then around noon yesterday, almost accidentally, I saw her at a window, the one far back in the corner of the *han*.'

Up to this point, Isak had been speaking volubly and fairly loudly, as if he were delivering a text he had memorized. But now he paused. And when he started up again, his words were very quiet; the sentences were truncated and vague. He said that he couldn't describe Zuleiha, not at all. It would be a sin to talk of her skin or the colour of her hair or eyes. 'Either it is seen, or it isn't, my lord. Either one remembers it for his whole life, or one passes that whole life in blessed ignorance, the way a blind man must live. A Franciscan who is said to have seen her abandoned his order and took to drink, but he never married. They say he said of Zuleiha that her feet were like paradise lost, her breasts more beautiful than any altar, and her countenance like the Promised Land.' At this point Isak stopped, got to his feet and walked out of the room.

I should eat something, Byron said to himself. He left the room a few minutes after Isak, and was surprised when he ran into him in the refectory; somehow he thought he would have wandered off again. Byron joined him at the table. In a moment a boy served milk, bread, and cheese, and Byron and Isak eagerly set about eating. Byron was ravenous, and the food very much agreed with him; it was as if it turned to honey in his mouth. The two men did not speak as they ate. But afterwards, they looked at each other and Byron got the impression that Isak had regained most of his composure. The grimace on his face, which was the stamp of extraordinary romantic suffering, had faded.

'Let's go outside for a bit, my lord,' Isak said, 'the air and the rain will be good for us.'

They went outside and stopped under the eaves. It was cold, but the rain seemed to have relented even more.

'There won't be much more rain,' Isak asserted, 'and I think that we can continue on our way on the morrow.'

Byron nodded. They stood there for a while longer under the eaves, in silence, and then Byron took a step out into the rain. He raised his eyes and searched for Zuleiha's window. He'd taken careful note of Isak's description, and he knew that it could only be the window on the far right. Byron continued staring up at it, and he sensed at the same time that Isak was staring at him with an equal amount of concentration. Finally he turned to his side, and his eyes met Isak's. Now Isak came out, too, and both men stood in the steady rain in the courtyard and looked towards the same window. The heavy white curtain had been let down like a closed eyelid.

'There's only one reason, my lord, why she would travel with her brother and such a retinue to Istanbul,' Isak said.

'A wedding,' Byron mumbled very softly.

'That's the only reason, my lord,' Isak confirmed. 'At the court she will end up with a vizier or a prince. That's the way it always goes.'

'Yes, always,' Byron groaned, as the raindrops streamed down his face.

They looked towards the window and said nothing for a few minutes. After some time, though, Isak added: 'Maybe it's better, my lord, if you do not lay eyes on her. I myself don't know if I should rejoice in, or regret the fact that I've seen her, nor do I know if

I would want to see her again. It's like when you have an unfaithful wife or a traitorous friend: you seem stupid when you are ignorant, but knowing breaks your heart.'

When he finished this reflection, Isak walked back towards the *han*. Byron remained standing in the rain, looking up at the window. He stood like that for a long while, not conscious of the time, and then he slowly directed his steps to the grove of trees behind the lodging. He did not enter it, however, but instead circled the building several times, the way the moon orbits the earth. On each round of walking, when Zuleiha's window came into view, he locked his eyes upon it as if bewitched. And suddenly it seemed to him that the curtain moved, as if someone were peeping out. His heart pounded. On the next round, the curtain trembled anew. And again! Yet again! Then nothing. And again Nothing! Byron picked up the pace. He walked as fast as he could. His lame leg ached tremendously, but he paid no attention to it. Alas, all was in vain. The curtain hung there as immobile as a flag in the rain.

When Byron finally returned to the building, wet through and through and totally worn out, it was already late afternoon. The owner of the *han* stared at him with a slight jeer on his face. He slowly mounted the steps, and, when he was about halfway between the two floors, he caught sight of a group of people on the first story: several men escorting three women. He felt as if he'd been struck by a bolt of lightning, and was rooted to the spot: he no longer even saw the men, or the other two women, although he knew they were there. The only thing that he saw was the woman in their midst – Zuleiha. The encounter was brief, lasting but two or three seconds at the most, but for Byron it seemed like forever. His eyes and Zuleiha's happened to meet for a second before all the members of the group disappeared quickly around the corner, into their chambers. Byron remained standing on the steps. He stood on the landing for a long while, like a victim of the Medusa, and then he slowly limped off to his room.

'You have seen her, my lord,' Isak uttered knowingly, as soon as Byron appeared in the doorway.

For now Byron said naught. He went to his bed and lay down on his belly, his head turned towards the wall. His eyes were open. He stared at the grey wall, or rather at a single point, a dark red point about two inches below a deep notch that extended horizontally across the wall to where his pillow lay. Apparently, someone had smashed a bug on this spot, leaving behind a red streak. Byron focused on this point, but in his mind he was seeing nothing but a single vivid face, a woman's face, Zuleiha's. From the stairs he had seen her for a moment, but in his mind he could more easily visualize her face than any other on earth, including his own.

In the brief confusion of the Bosnian company's retreat to their rooms, a few intermingled voices could be heard, and he was certain that one of them was hers, and that he would recognize it if he ever heard it again. It was unusually deep and decisive for a woman – for a girl, actually. And yet it was somehow fragile and bright and transparent. She herself was the same way, put together from incompatible elements. Tall and shapely, with a torrent of heavy black hair, with a high, broad forehead and breasts that looked massive despite being corseted, and hips as wide as a river delta: and then again she had a delicate mouth and ears, and small hands and feet, with almost child-like, delicate ankles and a neck as slender as a bow and a waist almost as thin. Of course Byron knew that he could not have seen all that in those few seconds, but he also now understood why the old philosophers in the Balkans had defined love as "a recognition". He recognized Zuleiha. Every previous recognition from Annesley to Sintra, had been a shadow and an intimation of this.

With a smile on his face, Byron rolled over onto his back and then sat up: 'I shall seek her hand.'

Isak said nothing for a long time – for what seemed to Byron a very long time. He had a stiff, mysterious look on his face. Byron none-theless thought he could read his thoughts: I'm a foreigner, a *giaour*, a limping devil, and she's a beauty, known to the whole Empire and spoken for at the court. I'm from one world and she's from another. Only Isak knows them both, and he also knows that there is no bridge or reconciliation between them; we are far too different, and that's worse than being too much alike. It would be easier if we were brother and sister. Isak is in love with her, too. He's resigned to the fact that he'll never have her, but he loves her, and he always will.

Byron was running through all these thoughts knowing that Isak was also thinking along the same lines. He waited for the other man to say something, for him to begin an all-out campaign to persuade Byron that all this was impossible, that he should not waste his time on it. He was supposed to dissuade Byron from this mad intention, and explain to him how dangerous it was and even threaten him, cautiously, ambiguously. But Isak remained fixedly silent, on and on, like a grave; like the sky; like one of the novices of Pythagoras. Eventually his lips began moving, slowly, very slowly, and they formed a smile.

Now comes the ridicule, Byron thought. But Isak smiled at him with boundless affection, and when he did speak, it was almost a shout: 'Well, I'll be damned! That, my lord, is a hell of a plan. Bravo! Woo her, and I'll be honoured if you take me with you as an interpreter and, if I may be so bold, as a friend.'

At precisely that moment, as if by silent agreement, they both stood up. They strode towards each other and embraced warmly. The hug lasted some time.

When they separated, Isak thundered: 'Tomorrow we will present you as a suitor!' And they both laughed, unreservedly, heartily, happily.

They spent the entire evening making plans for the next day, and their conversation was punctuated only occasionally by intervals of silence, but frequently by bursts of laughter. 'Time to sleep, my Lord,' Isak finally said around midnight. 'We will need to sleep, because tomorrow you make your offer of marriage.'

CHAPTER TWELVE

October 17, 1809

Byron was awakened by the thud of footsteps on the floor. Squinting through sleepy eyes, he saw Isak again pacing around the room. He's indefatigable, Byron thought. In his hoarse voice he attempted to bring forth the usual "Good morning." Isak stopped.

'It is a good morning, my lord but may God grant us a good day, too. The rain has almost stopped,' he added.

Byron propped himself up on his elbows. Indeed, the stubborn murmur of the strong rain had disappeared. Small drops still pinged rhythmically against the window, but gone was the heavy, opaque curtain of precipitation.

'Maybe that's a good sign,' Byron noted.

'For travellers, that is the case,' Isak replied. 'But whether or not it's also true for suitors, I don't quite know. Maybe it would be better if it snowed.'

'Why?' Byron asked with irritation.

Isak smiled. 'It's customary, my lord, in these parts to go courting at the beginning of winter. In the month of December, when the first snow lies gleaming.'

Now Byron was grinning as well.

'But this courtship will be anything but traditional.'

Isak burst out laughing: 'Yes, that is what you said, my lord.'

Byron sat up now on the edge of the bed, and Isak resumed his measured strides across the room. Byron fixed his eyes on the other man's feet. *"How many times have his feet beaten time on this floor"*, he asked himself. 'It's a miracle that there isn't a trail here, like in the snow,' he whispered, scarcely loud enough to hear. But Isak had heard him. He looked at him searchingly.

'I was just thinking,' Byron said, 'how strange it is that no traces remain on the floor after so much walking.'

'It takes a long time for that to happen, my lord. A very, very long time... Have you heard of Bonnivard?'

'I know the name,' Byron replied.

'François Bonnivard rebelled against the rule of a cruel count in the 15th century. The count had him locked up in basement of his castle at Chillon, in a small room, where the prisoner paced back and forth day after day, month after month, and year after year. From that walking, my lord, there were indeed tracks that remained in the stone,' Isak related. After a pensive pause he went on: 'Sometimes I think that the East and the West are not all that different.'

'So maybe we'll be able to woo Zuleiha then,' Byron countered merrily.

'Maybe is the right word, my lord. Maybe.' Isak was still very thoughtful. 'Visit Chillon sometime, my lord, when you have the opportunity; there you can see with your own eyes how small a space is required for the human mind to preserve its freedom.'

'The mind is a beautiful thing,' said Byron, 'but I am hungry.'

'Then let's go downstairs, my lord,' said Isak.

They dressed in silence.

'May I give you a piece of advice, my lord,' asked Isak, before they left for the dining hall. Byron nodded.

'Do not mention the courtship and Zuleiha in front of your countrymen. At least not until we have asked for her hand. They say that brings bad luck,' he added. 'But even casting superstition aside, I believe it's better for you for as few people as possible to know about this.'

'I was thinking the same thing,' Byron said.

As Isak opened the door, he whispered: 'First we go to eat breakfast, and then we will marry you off.'

At the table everyone sat together: Isak, Byron, Hobhouse, the other Englishmen, and their two Albanian escorts. Everyone was in excellent spirits. The rain was abating, and one could sense that the journey would continue shortly. There was a bustle of activity in front of the *han*, because several of the guests were clearly intending to be on their way that very day. Byron gave Isak a worried look. Surely she won't be departing, was the thought one could read in his eyes.

'Who is it that's in such a hurry?' Isak asked the innkeeper. 'Who doesn't have the patience to wait for the rain to cease altogether?'

'Ah, it's some merchants from the area', replied the innkeeper, and Isak translated his words for Byron. 'Little people in a big hurry – they'd brave hell itself for a bit of money.' Byron chuckled with relief, and the innkeeper beamed with pleasure; he apparently believed that the foreigner was laughing at his joke.

After breakfast, the men split up and returned to their rooms. Almost as soon as he entered his own chamber, Byron took a seat on the bed, but Isak remained standing next to him.

'The best way to do this is for us to take ourselves to Selim Beg just after noon.'

'That was my idea, too,' Byron said. 'The sooner the better, because impatience is beginning to gnaw at me.'

'Don't let that happen, my lord. *Sabur*,' said Isak.

Sabur – once again a mysterious word had crept into Isak's English. Byron was already compiling a little glossary in his head. He knew what *besa* meant, and what *giaour*, *dert*, and *sevdah* were, but he wasn't yet familiar with *sabur*. Isak seemed to have suspected as much.

'*Sabur*, my lord, is in essence "patience," but not of the usual sort. It is,' he went on, 'A type of metaphysical patience. In China they have a proverb: "if you sit for long enough next to a river, you will eventually see the corpses of your enemies float past." *Sabur* is like that, my lord, only not quite as harsh. Everything falls into place when its time comes, and if that doesn't happen, then it's all the same, because so much time has already passed. That is *sabur*, my lord,' Isak repeated, 'it is that and much more. But you and I would need far more *sabur* than we have at our disposal for me to be able to explain to you even partially, but in rich and beautiful detail, what the word means. Therefore this must suffice for now.'

And with that, Isak stopped talking.

'I believe I understand,' Byron added softly; 'at least in part, at least as much as I understand of *besa*.'

'That's enough,' Isak replied. 'Now we should get dressed for your courtship. I recommend that you put on the garments that Mahmut Pasha gave you. You're going to be a stranger to them in such a degree that something recognizably local would be appropriate, sort of like a cake that conceals the bitterness of poison.'

'My English uniform is dirty anyway, so that is the most beautiful and most proper set of clothes that I have with me.'

Isak nodded, satisfied. 'I will go with you, as your interpreter and friend, but you are the wooer. It is important for you to look Selim Beg straight in the eye while you speak, and also while he speaks to you. It's unimportant whether he understands your words or you his. It seems to me,' Isak continued thoughtfully, 'that it is not words, anyway, that will decide the fate of this courtship.'

Then they both sat there quietly for a time, until Isak suddenly clapped his hands and said: 'Time to start getting ready, my lord. Meanwhile I am going outside to get some fresh air.'

As Isak left the room, the door shut loudly behind him; but when he returned the movement of the handle was barely audible. He had not remained outdoors for very long, but Byron was ready. Isak looked him up and down and did not conceal his satisfaction.

'Splendid,' he said under his breath. 'You look splendid, my lord, not at all like a Westerner.'

Byron stood in the middle of the room as Isak circled slowly around him, so he could view him from all angles. Byron, clad in sumptuous silk and velvet, cut a profile that looked both menacing and meditative. He resembled the figures in Persian miniatures. 'Do you want to know something, my lord?' Isak asked, approaching him again from the front after sizing him up from all sides. 'You should have been born a Turk.'

'Perhaps I was,' Byron offered, 'but now we want to see to it at least that I get a Turk as a wife.'

They said nothing more until they were standing at the door behind which Zuleiha was hidden away. Byron knocked. The door was quickly opened. Isak said something to the young man who had appeared in the doorway – Byron made out the names Selim Beg and Ali Pasha – and the boy then withdrew into the interior. He returned swiftly and led them inside. These lodgings were, as far as they could tell, spacious. Selim Beg had probably requisitioned about a quarter of the entire building for his entourage. Byron and Isak were led into a large room devoid of other people. They sat down on a smooth bench and waited.

'So far so good,' Isak whispered. 'I had feared that they might not receive us at all.' Byron was just about to respond, when another door opened and a tall man of striking appearance walked in. He was bearded and dressed all in black, except that on his head he wore a white turban. With a stony but composed expression on his face, he greeted the two visitors with an ever so slight nod of the head and sat down opposite them. Byron said to Isak: 'Greet him, kindly but not obsequiously.'

Isak uttered two or three sentences in a theatrical voice. Selim Beg nodded again and said a few ill-tempered words. In a low voice, Isak translated them for Byron: 'He is asking what we want.'

Byron sensed that this directness was somewhat unusual; there had been no rituals of hospitality, no polite inquiries, no overtures of any kind. Byron was certain that the man knew why they had come.

'Tell him,' he said to Isak, 'that I wish to marry Zuleiha and that I'm asking him for her hand in marriage. Say it all with carefully chosen words, as if you were wooing her yourself, I beg you.'

Now Isak spoke for much longer, and Selim Beg acknowledged his words several times with a dip of his head. But the expression on his face remained nothing if not icy. When Isak had finished, Selim Beg sat there in silence for a moment. Then, in a cryptic, low voice he pronounced a few sentences.

'Selim Beg is grateful for your polite approach. It is very much the way courtships were conducted in the old days; it is a courtship according to the *tabiat*. Those are his exact words. A courtship that makes it clear you are of noble lineage, my lord, although that is also evident by virtue of your appearance. You have small ears, curly hair, small white hands, and an attractive face – and you look handsome in those vestments. That is literally what he said, and that all of these things are attributes of a man of aristocratic pedigree. For all of these reasons, he regrets that he must reject your suit. Zuleiha is already spoken for, but he also says that he must be forthright and let you know, that his reply would have to be negative, even if this she were not promised to someone already. You are a *giaour*. That, my lord, is precisely how he put it, and he will not give his sister away to an unbeliever. He said that, a few years ago, her father fell in a battle against infidels in Serbia, and that he would be spitting on his father's grave if he now gave her over to a *giaour*, regardless of his status. Since the death of their father, he has been both father and brother to her. That's all, my lord,' Isak concluded.

But Byron had barely heard his last words. The door behind Selim Beg's back was, alas, slightly ajar, and Byron was able to catch sight of Zuleiha herself for just a moment, when she peeked into the room.

'My lord,' Isak said again, in a somewhat louder voice. But Byron just said: 'Ask him what Zuleiha's wish is.'

'That would not be appropriate,' Isak whispered.

But Byron merely raised his voice: 'Just ask him.'

Isak complied, and Selim Beg's upper lip gave an almost invisible twitch. Once again his answer was laconic.

'She is a woman, and her wish is what I wish. She has no wishes of her own,' Isak translated.

Byron was quiet for a moment as he ruminated. 'Ask him, if it would alter anything if I were to convert to Islam, if I were to become a Turk.'

Isak was, apparently, not surprised by this question, but the expression on Selim Beg's face grew even darker in response. He added something in a voice that was tinged with disgust.

'What it would change, my lord – and these are his words – is his regard for you. As it is, he esteems you, but in the eventuality you describe, he would despise you. What kind of man changes his faith on account of a woman? Selim Beg asked.'

But now Byron was on his feet and almost shouting: 'What should I do?'

Isak looked at him, bewildered, but said nothing. Meanwhile, Selim Beg did utter something.

'What's he saying?' Byron asked.

'You can only win her over his dead body,' replied Isak.

Byron gave Selim Beg a caustic look and gripped the handle of his sabre. At that, Selim Beg also stood up and blared a few angry words.

'A duel with sabres, tomorrow morning at dawn,' Isak reported to Byron, who looked back at Selim Beg and nodded. The young man who had led them into the room came over to them once more, in order to escort them out. But first Selim Beg said something else. It was only when they were back in their room that Isak translated that final sentence. 'He said it would give him particular pleasure to kill you, my lord.'

The rain grew lighter and lighter until nightfall, but then it seemed to intensify once more with the increasing darkness. Byron and Isak had scarcely said a word the entire afternoon. In the evening, when they went down to eat supper, they were reunited with everyone, but the mood was nothing at all as it had been at breakfast. The mealtime passed in tortured silence, and the only thing that disturbed the deathly stillness at the table was the chewing of food in various mouths. It seemed that everyone was waiting to be able to take leave of each other. When they returned to their murky room, Isak prepared to light a candle, but Byron put a hand on his shoulder.

'Wait a bit,' he said.

A weak beam of dreary moonlight had managed to penetrate both the clouds and the windowpane, so that the room was not in complete blackness. Confused, Isak looked at Byron, who was pulling his sword out of its sheath with a solemn gesture. The sharp edge of its blade shone in the darkness. In the deep obscurity of night, the weapon appeared miraculous and powerful, like a magic lamp or a ray of white light from a star. They were both spellbound and stared at the blade, until Byron lowered it and slid it back into the sheath. Isak then immediately lit a candle. They sat down on their respective beds and the room once more descended into silence.

'You have a splendid sabre, my lord,' Isak said at last. 'But how is your arm? How are you at handling a weapon?'

'Never have I faced anyone better than I,' said Byron, in voice low and even, the way one speaks of blasé and indisputable facts. It was a voice from which any trace of arrogance was absent. Isak nodded.

'Selim Beg is very skilled,' he added after a moment.

'I would not have assumed any less,' Byron rejoined.

'Do you know, my lord, that when people praise Selim Beg as a singer, they usually say that he uses his voice as well as he does his sword. I myself have never seen him make use of it, but I have heard the way he sings. If his sword fighting is indeed like his singing, you will be lucky to escape with your life tomorrow,' Isak said in hushed tones. Byron made no answer.

Isak spoke up again: 'And people say that his sword is a force of nature, the blade as thin as wire, as sharp as a tusk, and as hard and lustrous as a diamond. It was forged in Damascus, my lord, and Selim Beg is supposed to have said of it once: it is as beautiful as my sister. There are swords, my lord, that are bloodthirsty. Believe me: his is one. Word is that he has killed many men with it.'

Byron again said nothing right away. 'Tomorrow blood is going to flow, and we shall see whose it is.'

'Now I will extinguish the light, my lord. Tomorrow we will rise before daybreak and the *sabah*.'

Blackness filled the room, and Byron whispered: 'before daybreak.'

CHAPTER THIRTEEN

October 18, 1809

Byron did not close his eyes the entire night, although he pretended to be sleeping. Actually Isak could not sleep properly either, but Byron wanted to give the impression that he had slept like a stone. It's stupid, he thought, dreadfully stupid, that what scared him more than the real danger of possible death in a few hours was the possibility that people might account him a coward for not being able to sleep because he was horror-stricken at the thought of an enormous and indescribable nothingness. Nonetheless, the night passed rapidly. To a sleepless man, it often seems that the cosmos and time have conspired against him: the night seems to be stretched and extended, the same way Ulysses claimed that Poseidon had made the sea surge up in order to spite him. But Byron's night passed in a trice. Maybe it's because this is my last, he thought bitterly. In the darkness, everything seemed gentle and familiar. Somewhere amidst the canyons of Albania, in a night as black as pitch, under a coarse blanket, he believed that he had finally, for the first time, understood Hamlet's words about a kingdom in a nutshell. Life and the world had always been out of reach, always somewhere far away, but now everything was here, within reach, in the unprepossessing room of a provincial inn.

This may be what the real poets call inspiration, something that he, as a poser, had never before experienced. Through the gloom blazed the words:

My own pulse I feel in my hot brow,
a sea of darkness concealing the goals of all my desire.

And somewhere beyond those walls are distant wind and rain.
There, where there's no love, or fear, or shame,
my tired heart reaches true peace,
a silence unmolested by wind or rain.

Hardly had the first harbinger of dawn peeked through the window, when Byron was on his feet. Yes, the rain had ceased. Now morning would come on fast, an almost spring-like morning, but Byron had no idea whether he would see it. Isak tore himself out of a leaden half-sleep and stood up also.

'No more rain,' Byron said.

Isak acted surprised; he opened the window, and the heady smell of crisp, fresh air pressed brashly into the room.

' It smells like *Jannah*,' said Isak. From the nearby grove, bird song could be heard. Byron girded himself with his sword.

'Let's be on our way, my lord.'

Selim Beg and his attendant were waiting for them in the clearing between the *han* and the grove. Selim Beg, like Byron, was wearing the same ceremonial garb as the previous day. Byron and Isak walked over to them. Selim Beg and Byron shook hands, while Isak, along with Osman, Selim Beg's attendant who was serving as his second, stood aside. A lurid red sun bathed the landscape in the purple of an approaching morning. The long rain had left the earth wet, but, even though the sky was still half dark, there was no longer a single bit of cloud to be seen. In a fleeting moment, the rising sun burst forth with the full radiance of dawn while the reflections of the moon and stars had not yet completely faded from the skies, – it was then that Selim Beg drew his sabre. Byron was immediately spellbound by its blade. He stood there serenely for a moment and then unsheathed his own weapon. The two men stood facing each other, their weapons held at the same angle and height, and only a metre or two away from each other. They took each other's measure for thirty long seconds.

One could say that the sword-fighters and their swords were both studying each other; and then Selim Beg lunged at Byron. But the Englishman was ready for him, and he easily deflected Selim Beg's first few blows. Selim Beg returned to his starting position and began slowly circling the Englishman with his sword raised and his eyes locked onto Byron's. His opponent returned his gaze and turned slowly on the spot. It was clear that the roles had already been assigned. Byron knew from experience that he, on account of his lameness, could not hold his own with an opponent of even average quickness. For that reason he had honed his fighting skills to perfection in a way that barely necessitated his moving from one spot.

Byron is like a spider, his English friends would say, and his enemies even more; he waits patiently in the middle of his net for his prey to fall into his trap, and then he forgives nothing. Now Selim Beg was orbiting around him like a wasp. He kept trying to land, but Byron was able to fend him off without much trouble. Isak and Osman watched the duel breathlessly, at their neutral remove. Isak was banking on Byron's sabur, but feared Selim Beg's aggressiveness; Osman was afraid that Selim Beg might tire, yet he was encouraged by Byron's static position.

But the sun seemed to be imparting new strength to both fighters. The more the dawn yielded to the ethereal and stately morning, the more forceful and frequent was the clashing of swords. The first thrusts came straight up the middle, premeditatedly, with the metal giving off hollow clanks, like stone against stone or wood against wood; then the fighting grew hard, swift, and intrepid, and the noise given off by the blows of sabre upon sabre had something like music about them, like bursting crystal, sublime and tragic and at the same time celebratory. Selim Beg did not sally forth blindly anymore, but Byron now had to invest ever more will and skill into beating him back.

In the observers, Isak and Osman, enthusiasm at the battle scene was itself duelling with the concern that each of them felt for his friend. Respect grew in them, nonetheless, for their opponents. From the beginning Isak had had a very high opinion of Selim Beg, but Osman's attitude toward Byron had now changed. At one point he whispered into his beard: 'The *giaour* fights well, although I won't praise his faith.' Yet now the clatter of swords was no longer the only sound accompanying the fight.

With the first signs of fatigue, the first heavy breaths, Byron and Selim Beg began attacking each other with words. Each would eject expletives and curses in his own language, and beads of spit would hit the other in the face. The words slowed them down, and Selim Beg charged less often. That was the moment Byron had been waiting for; and now he prepared to attack. He was only marking time until that moment when, after one of Selim Beg's unsuccessful sorties and his rebound, his opponent's concentration would let up just a trace. So when Selim Beg attacked, in what was now almost a routine; Byron forced him to retreat and made his own advance, for the first time. Selim Beg was surprised, as were Osman and Isak. Osman even unconsciously took a couple of steps forward, parallel to Selim Beg's withdrawal. Byron came at him harder now: swiftly, forcefully, and unwaveringly. These bore no similarity to Selim Beg's attacks, which Byron had deflected standing in one spot. Now Selim Beg, confronted with Byron's powerful blows, had to retreat stubbornly, step by step, towards the *han*.

Even the sound of the weapons was now different. Byron's sabre sang; Selim Beg's blade merely added an echo to Byron's. It was obvious that Selim Beg was fading. He no longer had the strength to counter Byron's ever-faster swings. But at the moment when Osman and Isak, one of them full of anxiety and the other full of hope, were waiting for Byron to point his sabre in the air and draw his arm back for a final blow, Byron slipped and stumbled. Selim Beg could scarcely believe his luck. The man who had driven him back to the wall of the *han*, pushing at him as inexorably as a torrent and cutting off all avenues of his retreat, now this man was reeling like a drunk. The arm holding the sword was no longer pointing in Selim Beg's direction, but was aimed off somewhere to the side, like a bird's wing, in an attempt to maintain his balance.

For a moment or two Selim Beg stood there calmly, and then he drew back his sword. Byron was in the process of falling, and the blow only grazed his forehead, just above his right eyebrow. Blood gushed forth. Byron lay there, his sword raised at an awkward angle, and Selim Beg stood over him with the bloody point of his weapon poised above Byron's chest.

Byron saw his opponent huge and impassive. Isak shut his eyes and Osman clenched his fists in delight. Byron couldn't look Selim Beg in the face; he diverted his eyes to the *han*, to the window, to Zuleiha's window. The blood was pouring across his face, and yet he continued to stare at the window, through half-closed eyes, in anticipation of the final blow. The curtain quivered, the window opened, and Zuleiha's head appeared above him. She uttered a cry. She called out something in a trembling voice, and her brother turned around and began bellowing furiously in her direction. Byron understood nothing of it, but from the motions of Selim Beg's hands he knew that he was telling her to shut the window and go back inside the room. She, however, didn't want to obey. Staring the whole time at Zuleiha, Byron propped himself up with his left arm and got slowly to his feet.

Now both of them were standing there, holding their weapons with their heads titled up at the window. Zuleiha seemed ready to obey her brother. She disappeared from the window but returned almost immediately. She focused now on Byron, uttered something unintelligible his way, and threw him a white silk head-scarf. The light piece of silk floated through the air like a falling leaf, and Byron caught it in his left hand. He gazed deeply into Zuleiha's eyes, then bowed his head and exclaimed: 'Thank you, my lady.'

Isak and Osman, meanwhile, had walked over to the wall of the *han*, and Isak translated Zuleiha's words for Byron. She gave a barely perceptible smile, with her lips pressed together, and then disappeared into the room and shut the window. Selim Beg lowered his sabre, turned to Isak, and said something. Isak was listening, and he translated. 'My sister said that she wouldn't marry anyone at all if he were to kill you. Those were Selim Beg's words. And if he spares you, then you must give up on your marriage bid.'

Byron nodded in agreement: 'He fought well, and he won fairly. Translate that for Selim Beg.'

Isak did so, whereupon Selim Beg returned his sabre to the scabbard and held out his hand. Byron stuck his weapon behind his belt, tied Zuleiha's cloth around his forehead, and shook Selim Beg's hand. As he grasped Byron's hand tightly, Selim Beg said something more. Isak translated his words. 'He has never encountered a better sword-fighter. You were close to victory, my lord, he said, and if you weren't a *giaour*, then he wouldn't hesitate to give you his sister's hand. You will go down in song, he said; a Bosnian song will enshrine your memory.'

After the morning's excitement, the rest of the day passed very quickly. Byron and Isak had breakfast with Hobhouse, who apparently did not find the white silk cloth on Byron's head remarkable, or, if he did, he didn't let on about it. The two Albanians and the English attendants prepared to continue the journey.

'It would be ideal if we could leave very early tomorrow morning,' Isak said, 'so that we could reach Tepelena before nightfall.'

'In time for *sabah*,' Byron said, and Isak nodded in assent: 'Yes, my lord, in time for *sabah*.'

After breakfast, Byron went back to his room. He felt like resting for a bit and then taking a walk; the gorgeous day was enticing him back outdoors. But sleep duped him, and he didn't wake until the late afternoon. Isak was lying on his bed awake.

'I slept like a baby, 'Byron announced contentedly.

'In these parts, we say that we slept like we were slain,' Isak said with a laugh.

'If things had been a little different, I would have slept that way, and forever,' Byron joked.

They both laughed long and hard, like children.

'I'm going out for a bit of a walk,' Byron said, 'while there's still some daylight. Tomorrow we'll be in the saddle all day long again.' He stood up.

'I would accompany you, my lord, but I've been on my feet almost the entire day.'

'To be honest, a little time alone will do me good.'

Isak expressed his approval. Byron was already leaving when Isak called out: 'They've already gone.'

Byron stopped in his tracks.

'The Bosnians have left: Selim Beg, Zuleiha, all of them, right after the duel this morning. Unexpectedly. The innkeeper told me that they hadn't even breakfasted, Isak continued.'

Byron shrugged his shoulders and went out without a word. He crossed the clearing between the *han* and the grove. It had not even been ten hours since he had been fighting for his life here, sword in hand. Now twilight was in the air. The sun appeared to be shining at the same angle as in the morning, but from the opposite side. The ground under his feet was noticeably drier, but the window above his head was closed and gave off a sense of mystery.

The shading of the blue sky was gradually growing darker. When Byron got back to the room, Isak was sitting by a burning candle. Byron took a seat on the bed.

'How's your forehead, my lord?'

Byron loosened the cloth, and Isak came over with the candle.

'It's not a large wound,' Isak said. 'It isn't deep, but a lot of blood has clotted there. When the scab falls off, you'll have a scar as a lifelong souvenir.'

'It will be a beautiful scar,' Byron said, and he tied the cloth around his head again.

For the rest of the evening, they did not talk much, and the little that they said concerned the next day's journey. They were both wrapped up in their own silent thoughts and for the most part avoided eye contact.

'Good night,' said Byron, as Isak put out the light.

CHAPTER FOURTEEN

October 19, 1809

'What does it mean to be memorialized in a song?' Byron asked of Isak before dawn was even close. Both of them were awake very early, like the morning before, and these were the first words spoken after sleeping. Isak's silence gave way to a deep sigh. 'In these parts, my lord,' he said at last, 'that's the only kind of glory – and it is more lasting than brass. Frail, and brittle and fleeting, is every kind of glory except the kind that song bestows. Books count about as much as stones in people's memory, my lord. The same piece of parchment can be written upon many times over, and horse excrement now falls onto the stone slabs from ancient emperor's palaces and medieval fortresses. Walls are constructed of the marble of old grave markers; people feed fires with books; but inside the walled courtyards, around the fires, songs are sung! Kings and sultans are quickly forgotten, but songs are remembered: songs about the strength of a man's arm or the beauty of a woman's countenance.

Only in Bosnia, my lord, have there been more than enough songs sung about unhappy loves, enough for the entire world, and yet still, to everyone in Bosnia, a pair of unhappy lovers means more than any number of Caliph Omars or Virgin Marys. The same people, who in real life pushed lovers to calamity, find themselves swimming in tears over a song. In these songs, heroes who have the world at their feet get their hearts broken by love; in these songs, a beautiful woman sets a city afire with a glance. To be preserved in a song, my lord, means being larger than life; it means being transformed into words, not into a written text but into a voice, not into letters but into a verse, not into a line or the rustle of paper but into a melody. If they should marry, these people, of course, sing nothing at their own celebrations; and if death overtakes them in the song, at least the song itself does not die.'

With that, Isak concluded his report. Byron was quiet.

'I'll go check and see if everyone's ready, and if our horses have been saddled,' Isak stated after a significant pause.

He left the room, and the door closed behind him. Byron remained behind alone lost in

thought and looking gloomy. He thought of Bosnia, this unknown and unseen land, and of the songs that the Bosnians sing. Not even fire can touch these songs, he thought, and that means they are real indeed. The poet remembers, and the poems will be remembered. That is as it should be, he contemplated; remembrance for what deserves to be memorialized, and what is forgotten was from the very beginning destined for oblivion.

Byron had to grin as he imagined the earnest, frowning faces of the first turban-bedecked men singing around a fire. The flames crackled, the strings of the *gusle* quivered, and their robes rustled in the wind. The song makes them sweat, and makes their skin crawl, and from time to time one of them takes a gulp of something bitter from a slender bottle, something that makes the tongue burn and the throat clench. A knock at the door interrupted these thoughts. Isak opened a crack in the door and asked: 'Are we ready to leave, my lord? Everyone is set, and we are just waiting for you.'

Byron followed him out in silence. Indeed, the entire company was already in the saddle. They all greeted Byron cheerfully. He found his horse and, before mounting, stroked his mane. In the resplendence of the first light of morning, the *han* dropped behind them like a conquered castle keep.

The sun was spring-like, the sky clear, and the morning warm. It's enough to fool a blind man, Byron mused; because only with eyes could one detect how far along October was. Such rains awaken the earth in spring, but now they are barren. Isak was riding along right beside him. When Byron mumbled something about spring rains as opposed to autumn rains, Isak understood him well.

'I know what you are thinking, my lord. In spring the rains wash away the snow, and the land and trees turn green. There is nothing more beautiful here than the first few days after the spring rains begin. It's a shame that you did not come at that time of year. Spring arrives overnight, and then the grass is greener than jealousy, and the petals of the blossoms are more fragile than butterfly wings. When the warm wind blows, it reveals one's soul,' Isak added. 'Meanwhile these rains wash the remains of life from the earth, as if one were washing a *meyt*.'

'*Meyt* – that's a corpse?' asked Byron. Isak nodded.

'I would have liked to see the birth of a spring,' Byron announced. 'In England we have no proper winter or spring. After a brief pause, he added: 'But we also don't necessarily wash dead bodies.' At that they both chuckled.

'It's that way here, too, my lord,' Isak went on. 'Some wash their dead, others bring them flowers, but both groups do what they do for their own sake and not for the sake of the dead.'

'So it is,' Byron said. He looked around. The countryside actually did resemble a corpse. Everything had been reduced to black and brown, to white and grey, and the blue skies were preternaturally lovely.

'I envy you, my lord.'

'For what,' Byron wanted to know.

'I envy you Athens and Istanbul: the whole south, to be more precise. Winter is on the march here, and it will not be pretty. The heavens will turn grey, the earth white, and all living things will be frozen. One can only wait for spring. And after spring, the order of the day is preparation for the new winter. That's life here, my lord, half waiting and half trepidation.'

Byron repeated Isak's statement in agreement. They were riding fast. Towards noon they stopped briefly to eat something and give the horses a short rest. From the *han* they had brought enough provisions for just one meal.

'By evening we will be in Tepelena anyway,' Isak said.

They ate while standing in the shade cast by a few trees. The trunks were still wet, and the shadows were short. The pleasant warmth of morning was now bordering on turning humid. The riding had warmed the men further. Hobhouse made a joke about Byron's white silk cloth, which he had not removed from his brow. Byron was laconic, though; the wound on his head hurt more than the day before. His face was covered in sweat, and Hobhouse ventured that he was hot because of the scarf. Isak whispered something to him, though, and Hobhouse fell silent. Back on their mounts, Byron asked Isak what he had said. 'That the white deflects the sun, my lord, and that's why you are wearing it.' Byron smiled contentedly. They rode for perhaps another half hour across level terrain, and then the trail began to climb once more.

'Now we are quite close,' Isak announced. The incline was not particularly steep, and the path did not become any narrower. The refreshed horses crested it easily and swiftly. When their little column had gained considerable altitude, Byron turned around and looked back. Far below them a whitish spot stood out on the horizontal greyness. The *han*, thought Byron, as he turned around to face forward again.

Time slowed to a crawl. The afternoon was as slow as the morning had been quick. The climb was gentle, but it seemed infinite. Even the horses seemed fed up with it. Fortunately we are very close now, Byron thought; and soon it will all be over. If it weren't, even I could start to be bored. The East has ceased to be full of surprises for me, and I once considered that impossible. My old problem: I'm alive to everything, and then indifference creeps in. I maintain no enthusiasm for anything, and neither can I hate. All of this was jumbled up in Byron's mind: In a few days I will be done with Albania and Ali Pasha. I will have satisfied the vanity of a powerful old man and quenched my own curiosity, and then it's on to ancient Hellas. Let's let the past jolt my soul awake a little if the present cannot manage it. But if I had lived in that past, I would have found it to be drab, too. Only the unattainable entices me, thought Byron.

All at once he was struck by his own ludicrousness. Take a look at yourself, Byron, he said to himself; have a look at your self, my lord, dragging yourself cumbrously around the globe in order to learn what you've known since childhood. You scurry through the world like the Wandering Jew, the Flying Dutchman, and everywhere it's the same: men, trees, women, and cities. Everywhere the same thing, and you also remain the same naive and arrogant Englishman.

He looked around: a number of men, a number of horses, bodies, perhaps souls: They live, they move, they eat, they sing. And time passes. Byron felt, he even sensed physically, the way the anxiety in him mounted. His heart seemed to grow heavy, like a weight in the left side of his chest. The oppressiveness spread through him. His hands were shaky and unsteady, his palms sweaty and slippery. There was a weakness in his legs, a pain in his head; and anguish, fear, and heaviness. He thought back to the severed arm he had seen on the road to Yannina. How long had it been since then, two weeks? Blood had once flown in that arm, and that hand had also held a sword. Today perhaps only white bones remained. Not too long ago, Isak had mentioned a curse common in these parts. 'If you curse a man here, you wish for the earth to spit out his bones. And everyone curses everyone else.' Byron had before his eyes an image of the earth spewing things forth. Of an earth that vomits like a person, ejecting white foam and bones like dirty snow. He felt the sour contents of his stomach climb to his mouth, but he suppressed it and swallowed hard.

'Are you all right, my lord?' Isak asked. 'You are pale.'

'I'm all right,' Byron shot back.

'We'll be there any minute now,' Isak promised.

'Any minute,' Byron mumbled. *"Everything is always so close,"* he thought. Then the calm was broken by shouts of jubilation from the Albanians at the head of the column.

Amazement crept across Byron's face, and his heart leapt at the sight before him. It was perhaps five in the afternoon and the sun was already going down. The silhouette of a city was displayed against the bluish-red background of the sky. It's just as it appears in books, Byron thought; or in songs. The closer they drew, the more beautiful everything became. He knew, he knew beyond doubt, that he would never forget this scene. A peculiar feeling of *dejà vu* had already come over him, even though he was certain that he had never before witnessed anything similar. Except in books. It's like Branksome Hall in Scott's writings, he thought. The palace jutted from a public square, on which Albanians were standing in rows, clad in garments similar to those that Byron had been given. Tatars with tall caps, Turks with fur-trimmed capes, two hundred swarthy guardsmen on black steeds outfitted with harnesses and saddle blankets. Drum rolls delivered greetings of welcome. The sun was almost all the way down. Against the dark purple firmament, the palace seemed tall and inaccessible. Taller than the palace were the tips of the minarets, from which the *ezan* rang out. *Akşam*, Byron said to himself. Night is here.

AFTERWORD:
THE MEN AND THE
MOUNTAINS

by John K. Cox

When Muharem Bazdulj writes fiction, he serves readers with powerful – in the sense of both heady and cerebral – but subtle cocktails; fortunately, like a stern (if urbane) mentor, he insists that we eat something substantial and make sure of our surroundings before we tip our glass. Bazdulj's works bear down on us with intellectual flags flying and we have to grapple with the plot on multiple levels of meaning, but this is all done under the sign of erudition, not sensationalism. Indeed his works are colourful, but one shies from saying they are exotic, because the last thing his native Balkans need is to be further exoticized in the eyes of Western readers. Bazdulj writes in the service of ideas, especially ideas mined from the history of his beloved, trying, misunderstood ex-Yugoslavia and its southeast European neighbours – and ideas being minted there in our day, as well. There is no more engaged, and engaging, writer at work in Europe today.

One of the hallmarks of Bazdulj's writing is his preoccupation with biography. What I mean, more precisely, is historical biography – fictionalized historical biography. This is, arguably, the raw material for "historical novels" in the traditional sense: famous or historically attested personages set against realistic backdrops with plots and details designed to move the merchandise or, sometimes, put oblique critiques of the author's own time or country into circulation. It is a subjective prejudice of mine, but I have to admit that I find most traditional "historical fiction" dreary; it tends to be neither formally experimental nor intellectually dynamic. Perhaps the problem is that such works claim to be trying to overcome the specificities of time and region and show their "universality", but their earnestness simply leaves them emotionally inert. But what if one believes, as I do, that every novel is universal, because it is written by representatives of the same species, and every novel is historical, because all are the products of a certain time and place even if they are set in the future or somewhere besides earth?

It turns out that such theoretical rehabilitation is not necessary, thanks to the works of Muharem Bazdulj. It is beyond the scope of this modest essay to give a comprehensive analysis of the way this fine novel fits into Bazdulj's rapidly expanding *oeuvre*, or to test the historicity of its depictions and assumptions against the standards of Byron studies. Let us just say that here, Bazdulj is writing about Lord Byron in a fresh, meaningful and adventure-filled way, paying homage to nobility of spirit and the galvanizing force of human beauty all over Europe. In Bazdulj's book, in his Albania and, by extension, his Bosnia, there is no pomposity, no name-dropping, and no wooden celebrities or Potemkin villages of historical relevance. We live through a brief period of Byron's life while he is on a journey through Albania, headed to Greece and Istanbul. The plot turns, simply, on Byron's growing friendship with his interpreter, Isak, and his love-and-duel-fuelled contact with representatives of an important Bosnian family in October of 1809.

Despite its relative brevity, the book is rich in detail. But the skies, trails, buildings, forests and fields (and even clothes and local words) are depicted so brilliantly – not for any encyclopedic or "ethnographic" effect; rather they contribute, like the omnipresent descriptions of the characters' clothes and sleep and meals, to a quiet rhythm and all-embracing sense of motion that is at once predictable and unruly. Things start, things finish, and they are all part of something bigger. On the one hand, we are lulled into a sense of sameness, and on the other hand we are in the hands of a sure, measured, and confidently developed plot that offers us irresistible challenges. Byron has come to the Albanian highlands from misty England, full of book learning and literary ambition and a Casanova's swagger, and he is bound for Athens and Istanbul; Isak has an even greater *wanderlust* and is as gentle and enthusiastic as he is wise, and he traipses back and forth across the Balkans as in a microcosm of the cosmos; lovely Zuleiha and her irascible but complex brother Selim Beg arrive from and leave for other parts of the Ottoman Empire. The Balkans, like the heavens and the (imaginary) guest list at the *han*, or caravansary, is not static or monolithic or impenetrable. People and words count, and they come to terms with reality; they sink or they swim, and unexpected events take their place at the starting line along with traditions every day. The Ottoman Empire feels here much more like a loose and far-flung confederation than a "scourge of God," and it is certainly more puritanical than any "painted East."

A second hallmark of Bazdulj's writing, and here one thinks of the non-fiction as well as the fiction, is the author's embrace of and elaboration on the word "Balkans". Many are the references to Balkan habits of mind and heart; religion, love, friendship, family life, quotidian philosophy, and, finally and very significantly, art and historical memory. These all play their part, naturally, in the tolerant Isak's long conversations with the sometimes slightly manic Englishman. The reader will likely enjoy this cultural exploration, the enumeration of which serves not only to enlighten anglophone readers but also to underscore a certain living, breathing trans-national cultural assemblage in the very pluralistic Balkans. There is nothing prescriptive or reductionist about this representation of Balkan culture; it is powerful but open and unpredictable. In the end it does not drive the story; people, especially the men, do. One could argue, though, that the one facet of this issue that is firmly fixed is the way Bazdulj situates the Balkans in the world of words and regions. Albania and Bosnia are not transition zones; they are not blended cultures, half-European and half-Asian; they are already the East. The words "Orient" and "Oriental" are almost never used in the book; the author uses the words "East" and "Eastern." Add to this the more conventional fact that Byron also refers to the lands he is traversing as "Turkey," and it seems that Bazdulj is decidedly stating that southeastern Europe, despite its name, is fully, and proudly, the Other. To this historian, this statement is a bold and valuable one. It removes the temptation to pick Balkan cultures apart into more Western and less Western components, and it acknowledges, as Danilo Kiš did in a famous essay from 1980[1], that the legacy of the Ottomans, of both the Muslim Turks and the Muslim and non-Muslim affiliated peoples, are parts of Europe.

Muharem Bazdulj has ably reworked, in his earlier writings, portions of the lives of historical figures such as the scientist Ruggiero Boscovich (Ruđer Bošković in his native Croatian), the dynamic American duo of Henry and William James, the philosopher Friedrich Nietzsche, and the occasional sultan or pharaoh. In addition, his novels, stories, and essay abound in homages to – for these references are more deeply felt than citations – writers whom he admires. These are powerful, enduring writers, and they include Ivo Andrić, Danilo Kiš, Mirko Kovač, and Ismail Kadare. In *Byron and the Beauty*, then, we have Bazdulj turning his attention to a Romantic, and romantic, encounter between cultures from two sides of Europe. In the mountains, Byron and Isak (and the boy-princes and even the jealous brother) *understand* each other. Inter-communal violence, victim complexes, spite, primitivism, tribalism – these things are not in evidence. Just how far the Balkans extend, we do not know for sure, for Isak praises the sun and ocean of Greece and Turkey proper so much that, at the very least, we know southeastern Europe to defy geographical stereotyping. It is in these mountains (are they really so uniquely cold and isolated?) that Byron and Isak connect. The book is about people, not fracture zones or clashing civilizations.

This is not to put too fine a point on Bazdulj's Balkans, however. Their legacy is challenging. His new parable of the cave and the reminder of Byzantine war crimes are platforms for the introduction of ancient disillusionments and horrors into our modern world. The oral traditions that tie honour to artistic production leave plenty of room for glorification of banditry and worse. But two literary considerations, I believe, secure a positive place for this book as a Balkan novel of ideas: The first is the way Bazdulj's work distinguishes itself from other recent, key works in literature by and about Southeastern Europe. With this novel, Bazdulj is swimming against the current in some ways, because of the agency and direction of the action: we have here a West European travelling to the East[2]. In many recent Balkan novels, those written under the influence of what one scholar calls the "new internationalism," it is much more common for the local Balkan narrator to leave his or her country and experience (and react to and cross-pollinate with) the cosmopolitan West[3]. Another recent study of the contemporary Balkan literary landscape stresses national differentiation in the post-colonial (formerly) Ottoman space[4]. In contrast to the trends in these studies, Bazdulj's Byron makes a successful visit (in human terms) to a place where cultures co-exist and share many values.

It is this idea of coexistence that brings me to my second and final point. Ivo Andrić, whose work Bazdulj has long embraced and even adapted,[5] wrote a powerful story entitled "In the Guest-House."[6] In it, a low-ranking Franciscan brother cares for a dying Turk. Although Byron does not die in this novel, he comes close, and he is taken care of constantly by the unusual local character, Isak. The roles are reversed in *Byron and the Beauty*, or better, jumbled up, but there are enough similarities to make the impact appreciable: Brother Marko's *musafirhana* (guest-house) is Byron's inn, and the earthy hosts are content to find common earthly ground while negotiating space to operate from the exacting political or religious hierarchies above them.

JOHN K. COX (*john.cox.1@ndsu.edu*)

1. Danilo Kiš, "Homo Poeticus, Regardless," in Susan Sontag, ed., *Homo Poeticus: Essays and Interviews* (New York: Farrar, Straus, Giroux, 1995), pp. 75-79

2. Lord Byron did actually visit Albania, of course, and he wrote poetry about it. Other real-life traveller's accounts of Southeastern Europe in general are numerous and have frequently been used by historians both to glean information about understudied societies and to interrogate the construction of Orientalist stereotypes in the West. Notable accounts include those of Edith Durham, Benedikt Kuripešić, Matija Mažuranić, Lady Mary Wortley Montagu, and Rebecca West. Recent academic studies have pushed research on such accounts, and those of East European travelers, into important new areas. See, for instance, the three volumes edited by Wendy Bracewell and Alex Drace-Francis: *Under Eastern Eyes: A Comparative Introduction to East European Travel Writing on Europe* (New York: Central European University Press, 2008); *Orientations: An Anthology of European Travel Writing on Europe* (New York: Central European University Press, 2009); and *Balkan Departures: Travel Writing from Southeastern Europe* (New York: Berghahn, 2011). See also: John B. Allcock and Antonia Young, eds., Black Lambs and Grey Falcons: Women Travelling in the Balkans, 2nd ed. (New York: Berghahn, 2000) and Andrew Hammond, ed., *Through Another Europe: An Anthology of Travel Writing on the Balkans* (Oxford: Signal Books, 2009).

3. See Andrew Wachtel, "The New Balkan 'Other,'" in Murat Belge and Jale Parla, eds., *Balkan Literatures in the Era of Nationalism* (Istanbul: Bilgi University Press, 2009), 143-153.

4. See Monica Spiridon, "'We Ought to Know Who We Are': Post-Ottoman Identities: The Feud of (Hi)Story Telling," in Murat Belge and Jale Parla, eds., *Balkan Literatures in the Era of Nationalism* (Istanbul: Bilgi University Press, 2009), 273-282.

5. See, for instance, his story "The Other Letter," based on Andrić's "Letter from 1920."

6. Ivo Andrić, "In the Guest-House," translated by Joseph Schallert and Ronelle Alexander, in The Damned Yard and Other Stories (Beograd: Dereta, 2003), 49-59.

The Author

MUHAREM BAZDULJ, born in 1977 in Travnik, is one of the leading writers of the younger generation to appear in the countries of the former Yugoslavia. He writes in a wide variety of genres, including novels, short stories, poetry, and essays; he is also active as a journalist and a translator. Bazdulj's short stories and essays has been published in *Best European Fiction 2012* (Ed. Aleksandar Hemon, Dalkey Archive Press) and in *The Wall in My Head* (Open Letter, 2009) alongside Milan Kundera, Ryszard Kapuscinski, Vladimir Sorokin, Victor Pelevin, Péter Esterházy and Andrzej Stasiuk, as well as in *World Literature Today, Creative Non-Fiction, Habitus, Absinthe* and elsewhere.

One of his short-story collections has appeared in English (*The Second Book*, Northwestern University Press, 2005).

Bazdulj is the author of six novels in all, including his most recent, *Small Window*. He lives in Belgrade.

The Translator

JOHN K. COX is a professor of history and department head at North Dakota State University in Fargo. His translations include long and short literary works by Danilo Kiš, Ajla Terzić, Ivan Cankar, Vjenceslav Novak, Ivan Ivanji, Ivo Andrić, Meša Selimović, Ismail Kadare, and Miklós Radnóti, and short nonfiction by Joseph Roth, Stefan Heym, and Erwin Koch. Cox's historical works include the books *The History of Serbia and Slovenia: Evolving Loyalties*. He is currently translating the Holocaust memoir of Simon Kemény. Muharem Bazdulj's *Byron and the Beauty* is his first translation for Istros Books.